ATONEMENT

EVELYN MONTGOMERY

For my children.
My reason for breathing.

INTRODUCTION

Publisher's warning: This book is a fast-paced novella and is considered part mystery and thriller with light bdsm erotica. Although all answers will be revealed in the end, the novella is written in order to keep you guessing until then and wraps up quickly as this is intended to be a short story and not a full length novel. If you're not in the mood for fast-paced, suspense, mystery, violence, light bdsm and short stories, then Atonement is not for you.

PROLOGUE

SEVEN YEARS AGO

ABSOLUTION.

A release from guilt.

For what I've done, nothing has the power to release me from my sins.

Penance.

An inflicted self-punishment.

For me, it's for a crime I'll never be free of.

Retribution.

Punishment, suffering, torture inflicted for vengeance.

A promise I silently make to avenge my family for not being able to save them.

Atonement.

Making amends for a wrong. A redemption, when I don't fucking deserve one.

Rain hammers against the windowpane as I look up across the way and catch the swollen eyes of my wife. My world. The only reason I have left for breathing when everything else was just stolen out from under us.

She'll never forgive me.

Fuck, I'll never forgive myself.

Tonight, was a setup. A trap. A conspiracy against the nation's two biggest threats, serving only one purpose, to drop us to our knees. To take Magnolia and me out of the game long enough so they could get their job done.

As my wife's lower lip begins to quiver, as tears fill her hopeless eyes seconds before her glare turns to stone, my heart sinks knowing we've lost, everything. But, I see no way we can ever come back after this. After being thrown into the pits of hell. She'll never forgive me for failing us. What's more, I'd never blame her for condemning me. We lost something tonight we'll never be able to get back; it all happened so fast, in a blink of an eye, and changed our world forever.

Rage fills the face of the woman I love. A trace of bitterness grows in her stormy eyes. She backs away from me in fury. My penance starts quickly sinking in between us, into the depths of my soul, as I watch her turn on me. On us.

"They'll pay," I hiss out as her breathing quickens and a harsh sob escapes her lips. "Every damn one of them."

1

PRESENT DAY

THURSDAY

11:45 P.M.

WANT to hear two truths and a lie?

My name is Declan Ace McClintock.

My profession?

Hitman.

My weakness?

Sex.

Now, I know what you're thinking. It's my name. Or is it my profession? Can't be my weakness. Or can it?

But as I look down between my legs, fist more of her long dark hair in my hand, and deliberately push her face down further until I hear a slight gag, I smile as my world goes black, my mind goes blank, and I couldn't give a fuck which two out of the three is the truth.

"Damn, I needed that," my voice rasps out several moments later. The dark tint of the window's now fogged-up glass blocks out just what's going on inside the backseat of the nearest car I found unlocked. "Mary," I halfheartedly sigh, content after my release as I attempt to pull up my zipper and push her back further on her knees. "It's been a pleasure."

"It's Magnolia, asshole."

My ears strain as they pick up her faint mumble, but my mind is already focused on my next task at hand as I open the car door and swing one leg out of the vehicle. I should care. Fuck, I know I really should. But you want to hear another truth? Something that might be hard for many women to swallow. Harder than it was for say, Magnolia, to keep in her delicious tight mouth just a few moments ago.

It's impossible to walk away from a past that haunts you every single day. A past, and a woman I might add, that I haven't come face to face with in almost seven damn years. Even after all this time, I can't deny she still gets to me like it was the first fucking time I ever laid eyes on her.

Standing in the dark alley, I turn around and buckle my belt, defenseless against her sass and a little speechless as a deep smirk spreads across my face and my eyes raise and slowly lock with her fiery stare.

"Jack Dawson," I wink, suppressing the laugh that wants to break free. "Next time, remember to use your hand."

I school her with the motion as my fist tightens and my tongue fills the left side of my cheek. But just as her shrill yell starts to assault my ears, I fling the passenger door closed, turn and make my way back to the front of the building. A disappointed chuckle breaks free from my lips as I shake my head and I can't help but feel slightly remorseful knowing I'll probably end up paying for my asshole comment later. Besides, I totally just feed her some Titanic bullshit. Both the name and the alpha asshole she thinks used and abused her tonight.

In all honesty, I haven't thought of anyone else since the day she walked out on me. I haven't *been* with anyone else since the night she left me. From the savage way she took what I was willing to give her just now in the backseat of that car, I'd say she's been living the last few years the same damn way.

But hell, what she doesn't know is also the one truth you still don't. A truth that has the power to change both our lives in only one week, if we let it. A restitution seven years in the making.

As I make my way back to the front door of the club, every inch of my skin suddenly crawls as I desperately hope, after all this time, she's game to try and find out.

The question is, are you?

2

12:08 A.M.

"I JUST FEEL like he never listens to me, you know?" I force my eyes to stay focused, trained ahead, and not rolling back in my head like they want to at the blonde's comment. "I try not to nag him; I swear I don't. No one want's a nagging, rambling woman to deal with, right?"

Present company excluded?

My eyes snap wide open as she looks my way for some sort of confirmation. I nod my head yes at the woman in front of me, pretending to stay interested in what she's incoherently saying as she takes another long sip of her cranberry vodka.

"I just really thought we had something special, you know?"

Her voice breaks and the tally in my head surpasses the bet I made with myself when this conversation started. Nineteen. The woman has said 'you know' almost twenty damn times in less than ten minutes.

Oh, I know, Blondie.

About as much as Rick knows just how much you can't seem to shut the hell up. But unlike the man that has to live with your constant babble, I'm only buying time until something better comes into view.

My eyes catch a glare behind the woman's head and instinctively I look up.

What do you know?

Looks like something better.

I stand up from the stool I've been keeping warm 10 minutes too long and button the top of my Brioni suit jacket, all while never taking my eyes off my target behind her head.

"See, you don't even want to listen either," she sniffles into her drink. But before I can think of a witty response, before I can feel bad for not consoling her, my feet move on their own accord, and I find myself quickly pushing through the crowd behind her.

Go call Rick, Blondie. He's used to tuning you out.

Me?

I have a one-track mind, and it stayed on your track 10 minutes too long.

"There you are," I hear someone shout at my right which slightly throws me off my game and definitely pitches a curveball into my selfish plan.

Turning around quickly, I grab a drink off a waiter's tray as they pass and pretend to be preoccupied. Turning my neck to the right, I train my ear to hear her voice and hold my breath as I wait for her to speak next.

"Silas," she breathes, and I swear I feel her warm exhale hit the back of my neck as a shiver runs down my spine heading straight to my dick.

"Where have you been?" Silas fumes. "We've been holding them off for the last 30 minutes. You were supposed to be here an hour ago."

An hour ago, Silas, she was doing heavenly things with her mouth in the back seat of a car that wouldn't be appropriate to perform where she's headed now. Center stage. For all to see.

But not if I can help it.

"I'm sorry," she stammers, as I pull my phone from my pocket and pretend to act normal. Human. Consumed by the tiny device in my hand that seems to ruin everyone else's world. "I..."

The same smirk I gave her as I left her on her knees in the backseat of that Mercedes pulls across my lower face. My thumb flicks across the screen in my hand, performing a task that would look normal to most as my mind trains and patiently waits to hear her excuse for why she can probably still taste me on her tongue, feel my velvet skin against her lips, and hopefully can't shake the thought of the way I left her from her mind. Just like how she hasn't escaped mine in over seven years.

"Never mind," Silas demands in a hurry as I turn to the left and see him angrily take her by the arm. "I told Carlisle you'd make the wait worth it..."

He starts to usher her off and my blood boils as I watch him manhandle her with force towards the stage in the center of the club. He takes a few steps and then begins pulling her closer, screaming something in her ear as I take one last sip off my drink and dispose of it on a nearby table.

Fuck it. I've never played by the books. Why start now?

Slipping my phone back in my pocket, I pull my Sig Sauer P229 DAK out from behind my back, previously shielded from view in the waist of my slacks behind my jacket. Holding it low, I crack my neck a few times to the right, and then slowly to the left, as I take a couple of steps in their direction and bite my lip to keep the perverse grin from spreading across my face.

This buildup never fails to get my dick rock hard. Something I hope Magnolia, my lovely estranged wife, will once again help me out with after I break up the reunion happening in front of me.

I have to admit, she wasn't devoid of affection when I had her face held down in the back seat of that car earlier. She also wasn't so, cold or aloof, when I had her legs spread wide before that, and her hot little mouth was desperately screaming my name.

"You want to play hardball?" Silas shouts as I come a little closer. "You show up on time! You give us what we're paying you for. You try this shit again, and you're through, understand?"

The second my Sig hits the center of his back he freezes. His hand falls quickly from her arm to her wrist, and I swear the idiot stops breathing.

"The only balls she likes playing with, Silas, are mine."

My eyes flick up to meet hers just in time to see fire rage in them like never before. That is, not since our one ill-fated night seven years ago.

In one swift move, the student becomes the teacher as she flicks her wrist, grabs his hand towards her, and quickly yanks it to her right cracking every bone in his slimy arm. She takes a calculated step forward. Her eyes never leaving mine.

"Try that shit again," she whispers, now addressing me as the bastard between us squeals in pain but knows better than to scream with my gun still pressed against his spine. "Holding my face down against *your* balls in question, and I swear I'll blow them the hell off the second I get a chance."

"You love it. Admit it."

"I'll never admit anything you want me to, Dec. Especially love."

She looks down at Silas and wrestles slightly with her dress as she pulls her pistol free and points it at the weasel in between us.

"Where is he?" her smoky voice rasps out causing my skin to break out in a sweat.

Fuck, I've always loved it when she gets like this. Fierce. Authoritative. Take no prisoners. Makes me want to make her see who's really in control. Something she hasn't let me show her since the night our lives were forever changed.

"Where is who?" the coward asks as we force him to walk closer into the shadows; the deafening music from the DJ continuing to blare through the speakers around us.

Hell, Magnolia and I have danced this dance a thousand times before. Just another day on the job with a gutless errand boy whose one bone snap away from breaking. In more ways than one. Yet something about tonight, something about the way she's acting has me thrown. It's a side of her I haven't seen since before the night our lives ended. The vengeful way I know she must always envision me slightly fades as she looks into my eyes over his shoulder. Maybe it's just a slip up from what happened in the back seat of that car. But as her eyes fill with a look almost foreign to me over the last seven years, I can't help but hope that maybe there's more of a future for us after all.

"You know who we want," she seethes, looking back at our man just as we make it to the black corner in the back of the club. "You know why we're here. The informant. Your errand boy. Where. Is. He?"

I put my Sig away, back into its temporary hiding spot, and then pull his arms behind his back and tie them with a zip tie I pull from my pocket.

"You can make this easy," her voice calls out as my eyes lift from my task and watch her gaze haze over just before she steps into our man and forces her knee gently between his legs. The prick takes the bait, loving the feel of her thigh rubbing slowly against his nasty sack. "Or hard," she hisses out next, a brief second before her knee jabs upward and the poor bastard kneels over in pain.

I roll my eyes because shit, men really are that easy. Kind of the way I made my partner on the force, *my wife*, out to look like earlier when we both broke and gave each other something we've denied ourselves for almost a decade. Something I know she'll never willingly give me again, ever. Thanks to a penance I'm still in debt to paying.

"Finish him," I hear my voice demand as I attempt to break myself from my torturous thoughts. Her eyes raise and lock with mine. A new light shines bright in her dark irises. Her chest rises as her heartbeat quickens and I feel myself start to get off on the look she's giving me. Crazed. Frenzied. Mental. I know, because it's the same look I have from the intense and violent streak running through my veins.

Glancing back down, she slowly kneels to his level and takes a handful of his hair in her fist. He yells slightly, but I'm quick to pull out my knife and hold it still at the base of his throat to silence him.

"I'll be nice," she purrs, and I can't help but grunt in disgust. She always was the perfect cock tease. Something I've unfortunately dealt with firsthand in our marriage over the past several years. But when you've fucked up as bad as me, you take what you can get when you can get it. I'd wait forever for another taste of Magnolia. And what's worse is she fucking knows it.

"One get out of hell free card," she seductively whispers a moment later.

"Please," the man cries. "I swear, I don't..."

Crack!

I barely see her strike as the butt of her gun hits the man across his fat head and knocks him out instantly. She wipes the sweat from her brow and lifts her skirt, putting away her weapon and leaving me standing, staring, with a raging hard-on for a woman I know I'll never have the balls to touch if she won't let me.

Ironic, isn't it?

"Pathetic," she whispers as she kicks his sloppy frame and starts off towards the back door. I barely have time to recover as I step over the asshole on the floor and pick up my pace behind her.

"Story?" I ask harshly as I catch up to her side and we both push through the exit into the dark of night.

"We couldn't finish the job and have the mission be classified as covert. End of story. They need to know nothing more."

She unzips her dress and I watch as it pools around her ankles in the dark shadows behind the building. My throat goes dry as

I'm mesmerized by the way she transforms, the outfit she has on underneath calling to me in a completely different way than before.

Fishnet tights. Cut off shorts. A sequin top that passes more for a pushup bra. As if her large, mouth-watering tits actually needed it. A lady of the night, and one perfectly suited to walk the streets around here. She unstraps her holster from her thigh and forcibly pushes it against my chest making my back hit the brick wall behind me.

"And Declan," her voice feathers across my lips as she leans in close, forcing us both up against the wall, and I swear my dick has never felt more painfully swollen with the need for release than it does right now. "If you ever fist my hair and force my face against your cock again, I'll bite it off and feed it back to you." Her knee rocks against my shaft and I suck in a breath, waiting for a fate that just claimed the dick of her last victim. "Bit by little bit."

She wants me to believe her, but I call bullshit as her eyes drop and she runs them with apparent thirst up and down my frame. She leans in and the world stops spinning. It's just her, and I, and our rising breaths as the air outside threatens to suffocate us both the longer we stay here, hiding in our own dark world. Pushing off my chest, I release a gasp I quickly try to disguise as she starts to saunter away. She looks back at me once over her shoulder and bites her lip, shamelessly checking me out once again.

"Little?" I yell at her back, just as she smiles and turns around, focusing on the road in front of her. "You couldn't handle what I forced on you at half mast, Mags. There's no way you can call it little!"

She lifts her middle finger and keeps walking.

Normally I'd worry, feel the need to protect her as she struts off looking like a prostitute rather than the most powerful woman I've ever known.

Normally, no one would get away with telling me they're going to feed me my dick either.

But the thing is, Magnolia has two things I want.

Her body, is only one of them.

A car pulls up to her side at the curb and she doesn't hesitate before jumping in. It speeds off, barely pausing as she slams the door behind her and leaves me wondering what the hell just happened, because fuck, it's been a long ass time since I was in my wife's good graces. If she's giving, she better damn well know I'm all for taking. It's a far cry from forgiveness, but even the biggest sinners receive absolution when they fully repent.

3

SATURDAY

9:45 P.M.

THE AIR in the room is electric.

Suffocating.

Racing. Stimulating with arousing thoughts as I stare into her eyes.

My arms cross over my chest as I shift my weight to one side and lean against the door frame. My feet crossed at the ankles, her power gives away momentarily as her eyes graze down my front, pausing halfway to my feet. She licks her lips in wanting. With need, and I can't help the smirk that fills my face as I take her in, teetering on the edge of her restraint. All too soon, her eyes quickly snap back up and glaze over with hatred.

Interesting.

"Say it," I hiss out as she puts her hands on her hips and now demands back the power that she just let slip. "Now."

She won't. She never does. Not when I need her to most. Not

when the demons from our past drag me under and threaten to never let go. They pull her under too when she thinks no one hears as she cries into her pillow at night, but I do. All I want is to hear her say the three words that she's promised me for seven years I'll never hear. *I forgive you.* But even if she was to surprise us both with that admission, I'd never forgive myself, so it's a lost cause.

"Cut the bullshit, Declan," she yells, snapping me out of my thoughts and making me forget all about forgiveness, her mercy for my sins is the last thing in the world I'll ever be worthy of. "I'm too tired to deal with your shit."

Her hands raise as she puts them on her sides and her fingers tap against her slender waist. I stand by silently, assessing how far I think I can push this. Push her. Before we both break. It's just a matter of time, and the slight fear I see flash in the back of her icy stare tells me my assumption is right.

We're both fucked because as much as we want to move forward, we refuse to let go of the past.

I wait her out a little longer, refusing to be the one to speak first. But as her eyes suddenly begin to soften, a sight I haven't witnessed in years, I find myself losing the damn battle. I'm a fool, hopelessly in love with my only weakness, and that revelation both excites and devastates me at the same damn time.

"Sweetheart," my heart betrays me, as my voice grovels slightly and I find myself pushing off the wall, miraculously being pulled closer to what I want most.

To what I'll always need most, above all else.

"Magnolia," she asserts.

"Semantics," I wink as I take a step closer.

"Define... semantics," she sasses, but her eyes lower again as she sucks her bottom lip between her teeth, and she studies me with lust-filled eyes as I come closer.

I bite my tongue to keep my harsh remarks at bay. The ones that want to scream, *"what we're fighting about is filled with no fucking logic."* But as I begin to take a few more steps in her direction, I know I'm wrong. If the reason we had to be fighting was irrelevant, it wouldn't hurt so much.

"The Declan I know has no loyalty to logic," she continues. "No sound reasoning. No intellect..."

"Mags," I warn, as the words that fall from her lips stir something inside me that I haven't felt in a dangerously long time. She's wrong. My intuition is what has driven me, steered me, and never proven me wrong. I'm not giving up now until everyone involved pays for what they did. For how they ruined us.

"...he shows no rational way of thinking..."

Her gasp is loud as I take my last step and reach out quickly. Grabbing her wrist, I pull her hard against my chest. Her eyes show no fear as my grip tightens and her breaths slowly begin to match my own. She's angry, furious about a past we can't change and a future we won't accept. Our heart rates quicken as rage simmers between us.

"It's hard to be rational when I'm always looking at you, Sweetheart."

"And you think I like working alongside you, Dec?" She taunts. "Save the dramatics for someone who actually cares. Last time I checked, that wasn't me."

I cock my head to the side and study her. She still cares, I can feel it. It's in the way her breath hitches as I take a step closer. In the widening of her eyes, before they drop and study my mouth. It's written all over her beautiful face. I can tell as she licks her lips and obviously looks like she's waiting to taste mine.

"You care," I whisper, as I back her up against the nearest wall. "Otherwise, you'd never have my back on the job."

"I watch your back because I'm paid to, Ace," she hisses as she tries to pull her hand free from my grasp. "Our little arrangement would be better off if you'd remember that."

"Speaking of watching backs," I rasp as I tighten my grip and refuse to free her. "Next time, watch your hot mouth when we're on the job. Your little slip of my name may have cost us. Tell me, was that a slip of your own logic, Mags? Your own reasoning. Because let's both be rational. I know you find it hard to think straight around me. Especially when you're so wound-up, tense, stressed, needing a release you know only I can give you."

She eyes me with bitterness right before her mask slips and I see the burning lust she's denying herself. She knows I'm right. She knows only I can satisfy all her wildest dreams. And I will. But first...

"Say it," I repeat the same demand from when I walked in the room and find a sick sort of satisfaction when I see her flinch.

"Why?" she hisses, knowing exactly what I need to hear as she moves in closer. "So it teases you with empty promises of a past life we'll never be lucky enough to return to."

She laughs in my face and I almost break, my control slipping at a rapid pace as she continues to attack me with the dark truth I'll never be free of.

"Oh, Ace," she says as she cocks her head to the side and studies me. "You really are a fool, aren't you?"

My cock betrays me as it stirs to life. There's something about her disobedient mouth and the feel of her body pressed against mine that has always been my damn kryptonite. She continues to analyze me as I stare back and attempt to break down her walls. But it's useless. She won't give me what I need, and for that, I refuse to give her what she wants.

Harshly, I throw her arm down to the side causing her to slightly stumble back out of my frame. She looks offended, taken aback that I would let her go so easily. But she's not fooling me. I know the Queen before me too well. It's a disguise. Her finest trick. A play to get me off the game so I don't see when she quickly takes her next turn and stabs me in the damn back.

"Better an irrational fool than to ever believe a word you say, Mags," I growl out in anger. "Remember that, when you're begging me for something you need right when you need it most."

"And what is it you need most?" she taunts.

I don't blink. I don't breathe. I don't swallow over the lump in my throat because it might suffocate me if I give it enough room. She's called my bluff, and she knows it. I try to play her, poker face for poker face, as we stand toe to toe in the middle of the room and we're suddenly thrown back to where we started.

Air electric.

Suffocating.

Racing. Stimulating. Arousing.

"Exactly what I thought," she laughs as she goes to step around me. "The perv at the club Thursday had bigger balls than you'll ever have, Ace."

She stifles a scream as I spin her around, quickly grabbing both her wrists and pushing her up against the nearest wall. Excitement stares me in the eyes. Desire trembles through her soft body before longing sets in across her breathtaking features. I push my hard frame-up against hers, caging her in against the wall, and feel her breathing suddenly stop as she drops her gaze to the floor.

Clasping her arms together in front of us with my right hand, I quickly free my left. Lifting her chin slowly and forcing her face back up, I wrap my hand around her throat to stop her from looking down again and force her head back against the wall, violating her free will and making her look me directly in the eye.

"What you think," I echo, throwing her words back in her face as I lean in and feel her quick breaths rapidly falling against my lips. "Tell me, Magnolia. What do you think?"

She goes to speak, but my next move cuts her off as my lips fall to the corner of her mouth and I hold them there, keeping her hostage and breathing her in with deep controlled breaths.

"Tell me, what do you think, Sweetheart, when I do this," I

whisper, as my mouth falls to the side, kissing the skin of her cheek before slowly falling to her neck. I get lost in the moment as I taste her porcelain skin and my tongue slides against her neck slowly, tenderly, with deliberate hot strokes as I savor every inch of her. Her chest presses firmly against mine in wanting, my mouth licks lazily up the side of her throat and pauses right under her ear. She sucks in a breath, and I smile against her trembling flesh knowing only I will ever have this kind of power over her. Slowly, I open my mouth and suck down hard, biting lightly and feeling my cock grow hard when I hear a moan fall from her lips.

"Does it make you... irrational?" My warm breath feathers against her ear a moment later. The word snaps her out of her haze as she attempts to fight me off, pushing and straining against my hold, but it only makes me tighten my grip and push her further into the wall. She surprisingly lets me, and shit, all that does is make me crave her more. "Does it steal," I softly murmur, watching as goosebumps break out across her skin, "all your logic, Sweetheart?"

"You wish..." she begins to say, but my hand around her throat quickly covers her mouth, silencing her before she can finish.

"You have no idea what I wish, Magnolia." My grip tightens and she instantly fights back harder, but I see the truth under her heated stare, and I'm fueled with the need to break it out of her. "Stop pretending. Because I'll tell you right now, all I ever think about, is you."

I step back quickly, before either one of us has the chance to do something they regret. Before either of us takes this a step further. Either by fucking up against the wall, the floor, across the table on the far side of the room, or worse, by killing one another like we both probably secretly have wanted to for years. Death is a welcome sentence for the hell we're still forced to walk through. Shit, after what we've been through, hell should be easy.

I watch as she fights for breath that won't come fast enough while we silently stare into each other's eyes. When she's finally regained some control, she yells, "Agree? You think I agreed to this? Oh, Ace," she chuckles. "I'd never agree to work the same job as you. A promise I made to myself and stuck to for seven damn years until I was forced to take this assignment."

I search her eyes to see if she's telling the truth but can't see through all the past that's clouding my better judgment.

"In fact," she says, taking a step forward as I involuntarily take a step back. "I'd never agree to live in the same country as you, let alone the same house while we're on an assignment if I didn't have to. You want me to stop pretending? Fine! Watch your fucking back, Declan. If I were you, I'd keep both eyes open. Even when you're fucking sleeping."

She pushes past me in a blind rage and I let her go. I relinquish all the fight I have left in me for the moment, as my heart bleeds wondering if she's telling the truth. Tonight, she won. But fuck, she'll always win. Which is undoubtedly the hardest truth for me to swallow when it comes to my only weakness.

4

SUNDAY

9 P.M.

DARKNESS CONSUMES me as I sit alone in my room. The only light is a tiny break in the blinds as it casts a small, bright, ray of unwanted illumination across the vast, seemingly empty space. The annoying tick of the clock vibrates through my skull, barely breaking beat before it ticks again and somehow succeeds in agitating me more.

On instinct, I reach out next to me and grab the small metal canister that has the power to take away my life, if I let it. Holding it between my thumb and index finger, I bring it into the small glimmer of light in my darkness and consider its power for only a moment before slipping it quickly into the palm of my hand and raising my glass to my lips.

The amber liquid burns as it coats the back of my throat. A welcome ache that lets me know I'm still alive. That it's not over. Not yet. Not as long as we're both still breathing.

We will have our vengeance.

When it comes to Magnolia, our story started off like a damn fairy tale. Once upon a time and all that bullshit. But once upon a time eventually ticks away until neither of you can regrettably take it anymore.

The click of the bullet loading into the gun barely registers in my mind before I find myself taking aim and pulling the trigger.

Bang.

I grin as the fucking thing falls to the floor in pieces. The clock a twisted symbol that I've been running from for all these years. The idea that maybe time has run out for us, for our retribution, but I can't let myself believe that.

Not yet. Not ever. If I can help it.

The gun in my hand falls to my side as I run my fingers through my hair and feel nothing but failure.

"Magnolia," I sigh. "How the hell did we get here?"

Pushing myself up out of my seat, I saunter over to the window and use my pistol to pull the blinds slightly more ajar. I numbly watch the street below. Waiting for a car to pass. A person to walk by. For some sort of resemblance of life to let me know I'm not locked in my own personal hell with a woman I'm afraid will be the end of me, if I let her.

My eyes meet the floor beneath my feet as I suck in a shaky breath and I find myself pulling the token of all my heartache out of my right pocket and rotating it around on my left ring finger. With tear-filled eyes, I succumb to the knowledge that the tiny gold band has the power to pull the trigger and put the final bullet in my coffin if I let her get the better of me, and so far, I've always let her win.

Crash!

My eyes bolt up just as Magnolia comes barging into the room and quickly closes the door behind her. Adrenaline kicks in, the nearly half-bottle of bourbon I drank earlier now an absent memory as I stride to her side and worry.

"Shhh," she whispers before I can ask. She turns, placing her finger against my lips and causing chills to sweep across my skin.

I absently reach out to her, my mind remembering a time when we weren't enemies. Her eyes hold mine captive, a secret hangs in them, but unfortunately, I'm too gone from her touch to see clearly what it is.

"Don't speak," she softly says. "Don't move."

"Don't tempt me."

Her breathing quickens, an electric pulse rushes between us, but I'm pulled away and glance behind her immediately as I hear footsteps quickly rushing down the hall. Looking back up at her with concern, voices I don't recognize sound off behind the closed door as she takes a step further into my side and I stare back down in her eyes with dread.

"They know too much," her worry echoes my own as her eyes beg for me to hold her closer. "I don't think we can talk ourselves out of this one."

"Since when do you back down without a fight?"

"Since I can't figure out whose side you're on anymore. Mine, or yours."

"Always yours, Mags. Always yours."

The voices get louder.

The footsteps grow closer.

"How did they find us? I thought the plan was foolproof?" I hiss out in the darkness as she takes another step closer.

"With our history, nothing is foolproof, Dec. Of all people, you should know that by now."

"You going to play games with that smart mouth? Or put your money where it matters most?"

She looks over her shoulder just as the footsteps reach our door and then suddenly grabs ahold of me tighter. I wonder if she has what it takes after all this time to do what needs to be done in order to give us any chance at survival. The backseat of that car the other night was a slip-up, at least in her eyes it was.

She got hers and gave me mine. But she denied me the feel of her kiss on my lips, knowing for both of us it would be too much. I guess after impatiently waiting for seven years, I'm about to find out how much more she's willing to push this to cover our asses when the enemy is breathing down our neck.

"Bonnie & Clyde," she quickly calls out as she eagerly looks back into my eyes.

"Bullshit! Bogart and Bacall."

I'll be damned if I agree to her demands, because those fucking morons, Bonnie and her ridiculous Clyde, got themselves killed in the end. The same goes for agreeing to something as generic as Romeo & Juliet. There's no way in hell we're going down in life like two love-struck teenagers who take their own damn life.

"J. F. K. & Jackie," she counters with mischief in her eyes. "That way I'm rid of your ass when all this is over."

"No time like the present," I hiss, stepping into her as the doorknob turns. "Your call, Sweetheart."

Her eyes flare as we standoff and the door pushes open. One more second and we're dead if she doesn't make her move.

"Mags," I warn, but she cuts me off quickly as her hands grip my jacket's lapels, her eyes glaze over and she desperately pulls me closer.

Shock rushes through my veins when her mouth crashes against mine. I never thought I'd get to indulge in the feel of her mouth against my own ever again. Now that I'm tasting her, savoring her, finding myself drunk on every feeling of her mouth-watering body pressed sinfully up against mine, I know I'll never be able to stop.

She moans as I push into her, backing her up against the wall. Opening my mouth and coaxing hers to do the same, a sharp intoxicating thrill rushes through both of us as her tongue brushes against mine for the first time. Restraint snapped, I pin her harshly up against the wall as the strangers enter the room and fist her hair in my hand, forcing her to give me more of what I've been yearning for. My tongue moves faster as it slides against hers, my bourbon mixing with her red wine and exploding into an addictive, manic, and slightly deranged mixture in our mouths. It's a taste so foreign yet oddly familiar at the same time, and I can't get enough of it.

"What the fuck is this?" I hear one of the men who entered the room say.

Lifting her in my arms, I push her legs open wide and forcibly crush my mouth back on hers as my dick painfully hardens between us. The prick's accent calls to me, something about it telling me to pay better attention. But with Magnolia finally back in my arms, I'm fucked for thinking about anything besides where I'm going to put my hands next. What I'm going to more than sample, relish in, ravage as my mouth begins to roam her sinful body.

"I thought Boss said the couple we're after are sworn enemies," the second jerk-off says. "These two look like they're ready to fuck right in front of us right now."

"Hell, let's sit back and watch the show then," a third fucker suggests. "She sure looks like one fine piece of ass. I don't mind waiting if he's willing to share."

Whatever hardness I felt building in my slacks quickly fades as I take in the bastard's last comment. Magnolia senses the change as my eyes open and lock with hers. She pulls me closer, her lips refusing to leave my own. She pleads with me with her eyes to be still, to not put up a fight, right before she bites my bottom lip so hard, I swear I taste blood.

She smiles against my lips, licking the wound she inflicted, never breaking eye contact as my hard body subconsciously grinds into her delicate one. The humor is, besides her perfectly soft body, there is nothing fucking dainty about Magnolia. A fact these bastards are on the brink of discovering as her hand slowly slips between us, into the waistband of my slacks, and she pulls me closer, as her fingers seek their way around the top of my belt.

"Harder," she whispers, loud enough for them to hear but only I catch the double meaning. "Like you mean it," she moans a second later. An admission meant for my ears only, as my cock in my slacks slides up between her very slick slit, making me growl out with need.

"When have I never," I grit out as I push up against her like she asks, spreading her legs wider until she groans, and feel up the inside of her slick thighs.

"Just one thing Ace," she winks, and I bite back the *fuck you* on my tongue as an evil smirk falls across my lips. "Remember to use your hand."

I groan as my eyes close, and I take her kiss harshly. Fuck, what I wouldn't give to really fuck her. Hard. Intentional. Thoroughly.

The kind of fucking that would take days. Not hours. Not one night. Hell, not even one whole weekend.

The rest of our damn lives. That's how fucking long.

"Come on pretty boy," I hear one of the jackasses behind me say. "Maybe he's shy," he continues as I hear the other two laugh. Magnolia takes her time, feeling around the top of my belt just as my hand finally reaches its prize. "Step out of the way, Moron," he chuckles as he takes a step forward. "Let me show the bitch how it's done."

Releasing Magnolia and ducking fast, I barely have time to turn before I see her throw the knife she's just pulled from the clip on my belt straight at the approaching asshole's head. It hits him straight in the throat, blood gushes everywhere quickly, squirting and covering the floor in front of him as he staggers backward.

Prick deserved it!

I don't waste time as I take aim with the pistol I've just pulled from Magnolia's holster on the inside of her thigh. One-shot rings out before the bastard to the right can even pull out his Glock. He quickly falls to his death just as the third prick shoots off a bullet that grazes past my left ear and barely misses hitting the only thing that matters most in my world. The life I just released when I barely had the time to enjoy getting back in my arms. If only for a brief fucked-up moment.

He dies slowly for that mistake.

I take aim and shoot him in the calf, watching as he yells loudly and drops his gun to the floor. Fucking idiot. Rising, I take a step forward and savor the taste of Magnolia still on my lips as she meets my side in the center of the room. He reaches for his boot, no doubt trying to pull a weapon from hiding, but I'm quicker this time. Shooting off another round, I wound him in the left arm and watch with delight as he falls flat on his back just as we both come to a stop above him.

"Stop, please. I beg you. I'll tell you anything. Just please..."

"Shut the fuck up!" Magnolia yells as she pushes him further into the floor, her heel grinding painfully into his dick. "Who the hell do you work for?"

"I don't know, I never saw his face. Only heard a voice. But I can tell you..."

Bang!

I shake my head before cocking it to the side. Releasing a frustrated sigh as blood pools on the ground behind his head, I feel cheated out of the painful death I was set on inflicting. One he no doubt deserved.

"I was going to make him sweat, Mags," I grit out. "Make him feel some God-fearing pain."

Turning, I hand her back the pistol I took off her thigh as she hands me back the one I felt her take from behind my back just moments before.

"He didn't know anything," she answers me annoyed. "Waste of time. Waste of breath. It wasn't worth it."

"Is anything?" I ask, shocking both of us as her eyes glance up quickly and meet my own. "Worth it?"

"*Once upon a time*," she sighs, exhausted from the dance we've perfected over the years. I go to respond, but she steps closer and stops me, all desire that danced in her eyes minutes ago now gone, as her hand hits my chest with a deep-rooted purpose. "Next time, don't waste so much time feeling your way to second base, Ace. Show me fast. Feverish. Not slow and sweet like you've never stuck your hands into places they don't belong."

She pushes on my chest with a savage force, handing me something in the process, before walking away and leaving me with one sick parting gift. I look down and notice the knife she pulled from my belt earlier, now covered in blood, and pressed deliberately up against my white dress shirt.

"Like I mean it?" I yell after her, but she doesn't stop, only shakes her head and keeps walking. "Oh, come back here, Sweetheart," I taunt, as I feel my molars grind together in protest the longer I stare at her mouthwatering ass walk away. "I dare you. Fuck 'like I mean it.' I'll remind you just how much I know how you love it."

5

MONDAY

DAYBREAK

THE TRUTH ABOUT A LIE IS, it's never, really, truly a lie, is it?

Most everyone's deceit holds a small amount of honesty. A little bit of yourself that could be true, if you let it.

So, what part of my deception is fabricated?

How far did I go to invent a cover-up for my dishonesty? A fact that may hold more truth than anything else I have said so far.

Are you listening closely?

The biggest betrayal is the one we inflict on ourselves.

The lies that restrict us. Obligate us to keep up the act. To behave in any certain way that we constantly struggle not to. They're a sick confinement, forcing us to carry out a death wish on our souls when all we really care about, all we really want, is to live free of the guilt from the one truth that's swallowing us whole.

My name is Declan Ace McClintock.

That you know.

But how far will I go to protect my illusion?

I hope you're comfortable, because we're just getting started.

It's a dangerous world we all live in, but my secret makes mine twice as deadly. It's a fact I've kept hidden for the last several years, even from my wife. The one soul I used to believe I'd share everything with. But keeping this secret will only serve to protect her as I work to accomplish an end to my penance.

That being said, I'm more likely to die from the show Magnolia's putting on in front of my intelligently placed camera right now, than from any asshole who's holding a grudge and decided to burn me in the process.

"What'd you say your name was again, handsome?" she purrs as she pours the cocksucker behind her a drink. She then pulls the top of her dress down seductively low before glancing up directly into the camera above to make sure I'm watching.

"Timmy," the skinny creep stutters as he answers back a little too jittery. "Uh, Ti...Ti...Timmy Walters."

Her eyes stay locked on mine through the lens as my cock grows hard and I watch her pick up an ice cube, roll it across her collarbone, and then slowly lower it down to her ample cleavage. Her tits are on full display, making both mine and Timmy's mouths water. I shake my head at her and adjust the hardening length in my slacks before sitting up straighter and increasing the volume on the monitor.

"Timmy," her raspy, sexy, phone operator voice rings out through the feed snapping both Tim and me out of our sexual haze. She winks into the lens, a reminder of which one of us is really in control, before turning and giving me a delicious view of her plump ass as she proceeds to cock her head to the side and study our next victim. The kid we went to the club looking for five fucking days ago. "That's short for Timothy, isn't it?"

He nods, excited and overly eager as she starts to take a step towards him in the center of the room.

"I bet you made all the boys jealous," she teases, as she reaches his chair and hands him his drink. He goes to take a sip, to stop his jitters, but she stops him by kicking his feet out to both sides and taking a step between his legs. "I bet you had all the girls wishing they were yours," she seductively sings, slowly lowering herself and taking a seat on his lap. I crack my neck to each side and grind my teeth together in envious rage. She lifts his shaky hand, the one holding his drink, and raises it to his lips; allowing him the sip she denied him earlier just as she leans in and whispers something in his ear. My fists clench and my knuckles turn white as I wait with building fury to hear what she says next.

"I bet they all wish they could sit on your lap," she suggests.

I stand abruptly and knock my chair over in the process just as her hand starts to travel up the inside of his thigh. I'm paralyzed with greed, standing stiff as a fucking bolder, selfish as shit, and needing her hands reserved only for my lap. My body. My fucking hard dick. Not his sorry excuse for anything resembling manhood.

"But you're all grown up now, aren't you Timothy?" she whispers, her hand reaching its prize and making little Timmy jolt back in surprise. I notice the pathetic, small bulge in his pants that wouldn't please a virgin, let alone a woman as demanding as Magnolia, and grunt in disgust. "What did you say you do now, Timmy?" she breathes in his ear, and I roll my eyes as the tiny-dick Timmy's hand starts shaking and spilling his drink everywhere.

"Software developer," he sputters, "F..f..for Nasa."

"Mm," she purrs, pretending to be in awe as if she didn't already know, right before she gives his sorry excuse for a cock another stroke. I roll my eyes and swear the kid cums right then and there in his pants as his eyes roll back in his head. "Bet you're the smartest man I've ever had, the pleasure with, Timmy."

Fuck this! I've had enough of her show for two reasons. One, all cock-teasing and pleasing belongs to me. Two, she's selling herself too low for a woman who's worth more than she'll ever know, and I can't watch another gut-wrenching second of it.

"Bet you could tell me things I've never thought up in my wildest dreams," I hear her say as I push through my bedroom door and stalk out into the hallway.

Wildest dreams?

She has no fucking idea.

With my room strategically located next to her suite, I stride the few steps down the corridor filled with a rage I haven't felt in years and try to calm my breathing. Obsessed, and entirely way too possessed with the need to be in control of this situation, and her sleazy peep show, I try to restrain myself before I barge through the door and do something I know I'll never actually regret, but may have to answer for later.

Incoherent mumbles are all I can make out as I pull my Sig from its holster, my right leg instinctively raises, and without thinking, I kick in the damn door between us. Their forms are hard to make out in the darkness as my eyes take some time to adjust after coming from the light, but thanks to our little buddy Timmy, I catch his fearful jump as he catapults Magnolia off his lap and hurries to a corner in the far left of the room. Taking aim, I momentarily catch Mag's disapproval in the sway of her body as she puts her hands on her hips and no doubt rolls her eyes with displeasure.

Entering the space in two strides, I kick the door behind me closed, and tell myself to fucking breathe. The only guy getting his dick rubbed tonight is me, and it's time both Timmy and Magnolia understand that.

"What are you going to do now, Ace?" she huffs as she squares her shoulders and turns around to lock eyes with our target. "If you shoot him, he won't give us what we need."

"Looks like he got more than he needed while you were

practically riding his dick, Sweetheart." I cock the Sig and watch as the front of Timmy's slacks grow wet. Fucking great! But I guess I can't expect a guy named Timmy to not piss himself when he's facing a loaded gun, can I?

Magnolia never takes her eyes off our man and slowly lets out a few tisks of disapproval as I take a couple of steps closer to her side. "What are we going to do with him now," she sighs, as her gaze falls, and she takes in his pathetic disgrace.

I can't deny it, I kind of feel bad for the kid. Shaking uncontrollably, eyes bugging out of his head, twitching around like a meth addict, he's giving himself whiplash from glancing back and forth between us in fear, and I can't blame him. If I were a weaker man, I'd probably piss myself too. Good thing I've never been anything close to weak, a fact I make known as I raise the gun and aim it straight at the center of his skull. The way he starts convulsing with panic thrills me, and I swear he's one second away from a heart attack, that, let's face it, he'd be better off facing than the two unforgiving souls in front of him.

"Well," I hiss, keeping my aim straight at the fucker's head. "I'd say his limp dick needs no resuscitation from you, Sweetheart."

"For fuck's sake, Ace..."

Bang!

Both little Timmy and Mags jolt as I pull the trigger and a small piece of plaster falls from the ceiling into the middle of the room.

"What the hell was that about?" she asks as I look back at Timmy. His eyes dart from side to side in an obvious attempt to plan a break away now that he fully understands just how much his life is in our fucked-up hands.

I cock my Sig again and take a step towards our man. I'll play fair for a moment, a nice attempt to let him know he's an idiot if his tiny little brain, which no doubt matches the size of his dick, thinks he has a chance at surviving any kind of escape.

"You have a nasty habit of repeating facts you shouldn't in

front of company, Sweetheart," I remind Magnolia, addressing the way she let my name just slip from her lips. "I've warned you before. Don't push me again."

"Push you," she exclaims, making me sigh loudly in annoyance. "Push you, Dec..."

Bang!

"What the fuck!" Timmy screams as a bullet pierces his left leg. His yells echo off the wall seconds later and show no signs of stopping as Magnolia rolls her eyes in annoyance.

"Care to explain now?" she hisses as I push past her and grab little Timmy by his hair.

"Don't hurt me! Please, I'll tell you anything you want. I swear it," he cries, as spit flies from his mouth and if it's possible, I swear the NASA dweeb pisses himself a little more in his pants. Flinging him up against the back wall, my palm closes tightly around his neck as I squeeze his throat and finally succeed in stopping his whimpers.

"We don't want to hurt you, Tim," I seethe.

I release his throat slightly so he can take a breath and wait for him to respond. I can feel the heat of Magnolia at my back and her close presence steals my train of thought momentarily as I fight with myself to focus, to not get lost in her. Not here. Not now. Not when we need this little prick to agree to help us if we're going to accomplish this job.

"Then, wh...wha...what do you want?" he stammers.

"We need you to do us a favor," Magnolia answers for me in a hushed tone.

His eyes grow wide. "A favor," he cries as if he's already made his decision, and it's undoubtedly no. I tighten my grip on his throat and push the tip of my gun against his wounded leg, grinding and pushing in with only a little force. It does the trick as fresh tears form in Timmy's eyes and I swear he believes he's about to take his last breath.

"Yes, Timothy," Magnolia purrs in her sex-kitten voice that always seems to do the trick. "A favor."

"We need you to locate some information stored on SCIFs isolated networks," I explain. "We'd do it ourselves, but as I'm sure you know, these networks are air-gapped. Impenetrable. Only accessible from the inside."

I release my grip on his neck slightly so he can respond, only to have my annoyance grow as he gasps for air and leaves us hanging several aggravating seconds too long.

"I...I...can't," he insists. "I'm not authorized at SCIF."

A tight squeeze of my fist cuts off his air supply once again before he can say another word. I intend to end him, he's useless to us now, but Magnolia stops me as she places a hand on my shoulder and I find myself temporarily powerless under her touch. Releasing my hold, I allow him air but keep him held hostage against the wall so Magnolia can attempt to show me just why he's not disposable to us now.

"You forget who you're talking to, Timothy," she asserts. "Don't worry about authorization. Can you access the network if we can get you permission to enter the facility?"

"Absolutely, but..."

"We need you to retrieve satellite information for Beijing and Moscow," I inform him as I cut off his reply harshly.

"But...," the fool stammers again.

"We'll also need information for Shanghai and the Khamovniki District," I continue. "Is this going to be a problem?"

His eyes flash between Magnolia and mine. Frantic. Indecisive. Afraid to say yes, but more terrified to reply no.

Tightening my grip, I take a single step into his frame and see his indecision waver as he quickly starts to fall over to the right side of his annoyingly slow decision-making.

Good boy, Tim.

"This wasn't a request," I hiss. "You'll do as we ask, or..."

"I... I'll do it," he quickly stutters, saving both Magnolia and me from the pleasure of ripping him apart any further. Limb by slimy limb if I had my choice.

"Tomorrow," Mags demands. "By Midnight." His eyes grow wide as his brain registers what he just heard her say. "Is that going to be a problem?"

"No," he insists in a hurry. "No problem."

I back away from him just as Magnolia takes a step backward as well. His body falls limp to the floor as he grabs his wounded leg and starts to cry. Three men enter the room behind us and rush to attend to his injury. No doubt watching through the two-way mirror across the room and waiting, as per orders from the higher-ups at the FBI. Timmy starts to sob uncontrollably below us, yet, oddly, no noise comes from his pathetic lips as he chokes on his fear. He's finally realizing he just cheated death tonight, only to face a fate far worse tomorrow if our mission fails. Shaking my head, I turn and put his misfortune behind me as I make my way towards the door.

"Russia?" Magnolia whispers between us as we walk out of the room and the medics tend to damage that could've been worse if we didn't get little Timmy's cooperation. "I thought the only target was China. What the hell are you not telling me, Dec?"

"Since when do we share secrets, Sweetheart?" I hiss, not wanting to share my deepest secret yet, not until I am absolutely sure I won't fail her again. "Last time I checked, it was the last time I had you in my bed."

"Sleeping with the enemy has its perks, Ace," she deadpans. "But that was back when I trusted you, back when I trusted us."

"That's your mistake, Mags. Not mine."

"What?" she demands furiously, forcing me to stare her straight in the eyes. "The sex? Or the trust?"

"Don't tell me you're one of those girls?" I tease, provoking her when I damn well know better. "You don't believe in one without the other. Right, Sweetheart?"

"Love, Dec," she firmly states. "You can't have love without trust. Not sex."

"Then I guess we're in the clear." She goes to quickly respond but I cut her off. "Oh, that's right. You won't admit to love, will you? At least, not where I'm concerned."

Her icy stare pins me in place as my heart races, wishing she'd take the bait and tell me off. Better yet, I wish she'd take the bait and admit it. Finally. Once and for all. Because what we had was more than any lucky bastard could ever call love.

"Are you finished?" she finally whispers, but a moment later I swear my sight momentarily forsakes me as I witness a little bit of the constant fight in her eyes leave her body. It's a crack. A break in her normal bulletproof barrier. Not an admittance by any means, but I'll take it.

"Never," my voice cracks as I shake my head in disbelief, amazed that she can think any different. I watch as her eyes begin to fill with heartache and my breath instantly catches in my throat.

What the hell is this?

Sideswiped by the change, my mouth speaks before my brain can tell myself not to and I force myself to ask, "Are you?"

My words stun her for a moment too long. She's warring with herself, trying to decide how best to respond. A first maybe for Magnolia since the night it happened. She blinks, and just that one gesture makes my heart hopeful. She bites her bottom lip and looks to the floor. When her eyes lift a couple of heartbeats later, tears fill the back of them and every reason I have to fight with her dies as I watch one lone tear drop slowly down her soft cheek.

"Clean up your mess," she whispers before I can speak; the double meaning behind her words isn't lost on me. "We'll regroup at 2100." I turn, defeated as I make my way back towards my room, needing to put some space between us and process where this is going. Where we're going. In all this mess. I stop in my tracks when I hear her call out.

"Ace, to answer your question, I believe you're hiding something from me. Question is, how far are you going to let me play you until I find out what it is?"

6

TUESDAY

9 P.M.

ONE THING MAGNOLIA said Sunday burns, grabbing ahold of every last space in my mind, and threatens to never let go as we sit side-by-side in my car and wait.

"...you've stuck your hands' places they don't belong."

It's a truth I've been trying to outrun for seven long years.

We've been sitting here close to an hour now, and I still can't get the venom from those words out of my mind. I look down at my fists, clenched tight in my lap, knuckles white as memories resurface and I find it utterly impossible to stop thinking about all the blood my hands have spilled since then. All the life I've taken. All the life I can never give back. The life I'd give anything to replace. Anything to resurrect. No matter what I was asked to sacrifice in exchange.

"He's going to fuck it up, I know it," Magnolia's whisper

breaks through my self-pity, pulling me back to the present as I glance over at her in the darkness. "Fucking Timmy. Why'd our only hope have to be a spineless computer freak who wouldn't know the basics of how to tug on his own dick to get off?"

A grin spreads across my lips because she just pegged him perfectly. Shrugging my shoulders, I look back straight ahead and wait for our signal as the quiet threatens to bring back with it the nightmare I'd give anything to escape. Unfortunately for me, that requires luck. Something I haven't had when it comes to outrunning *our* demons. Something, I'm hoping finally changes. That is, if Timmy follows through for us tonight.

"What?" I force a laugh. "Did you actually think this mission could be accomplished any other way? With a man instead of a boy?" I wait for her response. For the quick wit of her addictive tongue. When it doesn't come, I go on. "Real men have already mastered the games boys can't stop playing, Mags. We grow tired with the sport; move onto more - amusing conquests. A man's too busy ruling his world. Taking his place as a King. Boys, well they're still trying to figure out what world they fit into and losing at the games that keep them there. Our friend Timmy is a prime example."

She turns and looks at me and I can't help but do the same, staring back in the eyes of the one woman who will always hold more power over me than she knows. A woman that can call bullshit on every word I've just said because I've gladly lost every game we've started since the day we met just to keep her in my world. And what's more, I'll go on losing, even just for a chance, and even if she never lets me back into her heart. Her eyes cast down between us as the air becomes almost too thick to breathe, the pull between us too strong, like always. It's an invisible wire that's always had us more tangled than free.

"How's that going for you," she whispers, as her soft eyes look up and hold mine. "Constantly losing the game that's keeping you here?"

I swallow harshly as my teeth grind together with such force I swear they'll break. "I know what world I fit into, Sweetheart," I snap. "If you've forgotten your place in it, I'll be happy to remind you."

She closes her eyes as a sinister smile spreads across her dark face, the pull between us beginning to snap as reality sets in. "Mm, broken promises, mediocre sex, hell on earth tormenting me daily." Her eyes open as fire fills my veins. "I think I'll pass, Ace."

Before I can respond, motion across the lot catches my attention and has me quickly moving to exit the vehicle. With my hand on the door handle, I look back at Magnolia and say, "Mediocre sex my ass, Mags. Your pussy's never been owned more than when I'm the one fucking it. That's a certifiable fact."

Climbing out of the car, I slam the door and leave any bitchy reply she can think of inside the vehicle with her, where it belongs, instead of pulling me down into hell like she always intends. The cold night air is a welcome contrast to the inferno raging inside me. A fire that I notice slowly begins to simmer as I look back in the car and see Magnolia at a loss for words.

Finally.

But before I can enjoy the break in her armor too long, motion across the way catches my eye again; this time Magnolia notices too as she exits the car and we both take a couple of calculated steps to meet up at the front of the hood.

"One more signal and we're going in," I whisper with bated breath, knowing Magnolia's right. Timmy is going to fuck this up, and when he does, it'll mean more innocent blood spilled on my hands that I could've tried to stop.

We wait, holding our breath as the venom we've just spread between us inevitably seeps in. The tension between us threatens to smother us. The past will always pull us back into hell the longer we leave shit unsaid. It's a dangerous threat to our control, our ability to finish the job, a brewing disaster that needs to be dealt with. But now is not the time. Wrapped up in thought, I almost miss the third signal a second later, but it catches both our eyes, and we quickly take off towards the back entrance.

"Fucking Timmy," Magnolia seethes just as I press the button on my earpiece and speak into the mic.

"Cut the hallway and rear cameras at building two."

"10. 4," our man responds. One of four actually, sitting in the van across the street and backing us up because we all feared Timmy wouldn't be able to get through this one tiny task without screwing it up somehow. "Camera 3 is down. Camera 4, 5 & 6 disabled. You're good to go."

Using our stolen IDs to enter the building, I keep my hand rested on my gun and go first, Magnolia follows directly behind me, waiting for me to signal she's in the clear. With a brief nod, I move out of her way and let her take the lead as we quickly walk down the bright hallway.

When we reach the end, she glances around the corner and rolls her eyes.

"You're up, Ace. Looks like my show's been given an intermission until later," she sighs in annoyance as she falls back against the nearest wall.

Well, shit, I wasn't expecting this, but with all the underlying fury running through my veins, I'm game to put on one hell of a performance. I quietly put my gun away for the moment, run my fingers through my hair and flip a switch in my head as I take a step around the corner.

The pretty little receptionist sits quietly behind her desk. She's here way too late and catching us both off guard. Lifting her head, she bashfully smiles, obviously nervous, before sitting up in her chair and glancing at the phone on her desk. I can tell she's wondering if she needs to call security. See if I'm authorized to be here, because, in reality, no one is. But as she looks back up, and her cheeks flush an adorable shade of pink as I come a little closer, my bets on the fact that little Goldilocks here won't say a damn word as she quickly glances back down into her lap. Her flushed, flustered demeanor is a dead giveaway. Taking a few more steps in her flustered direction, I know there is no way in hell she'll be picking up the phone to out me, authorization be damned.

"Excuse me," I smile, but she still doesn't lookup. "Miss, I'm sorry, but I think I'm lost." Her eyes finally flutter up to mine, a darker shade of pink dusting her cheeks as I take my final step to her desk and flash her my deepest, sexiest grin. "Do you think you can help me?"

My question startles her, and she looks behind each shoulder wondering if she'll get caught, or worse, if maybe this is a setup. When her eyes find mine again, she clears her throat and sits up a little straighter.

"Only authorized personnel are allowed through here, Sir."

The way she says "Sir" should have my balls tightening desperately needing a release they haven't had in far too long, but surprisingly - it doesn't. To any other red-blooded man, she'd be considered drop-dead gorgeous, but not me. Not when everything my soul will always crave is standing just a few feet away around the corner.

"I just received authorization," I lie, but she doesn't take the bait. "But, God," I stammer as I lean in against the top of her desk. "Like an idiot, I lost my..." clicking my fingers together once, twice, three times, acting like a damn fool, kind of like our friend Timmy, I smile as I silently beg for her to have mercy on me.

Because, let's face it, we all know there's nothing a girl wants more than to help a defenseless boy out in his time of need.

"...key," she finally finishes for me.

"That's right," I whisper, as I smile, lean in further and brush her hair back behind her ear. "Key."

Her breath catches in her throat just as her eyes grow wide

from my brazen touch. In fact, in two more seconds, I'm guessing I'm going to have to remind Goldilocks here to continue to breathe if I don't back away soon. So, giving her some much-needed space, I shove my hands in my pockets and lean away from the shocked look on her face, knowing even before she does, that she'll let my error slide.

Truth be told, little girls like to play the same games as little boys, and I'm entirely uninterested and slightly bored being able to call the shots while standing here, waiting for her to say something next.

"I don't think..."

"Sandy Winslow," I say, reading her name tag and making her look me in the eye. "Short for Sandra right." She doesn't respond.

Fine, Sandra, I'll bite and play along.

"Sandy," I roll her name on my tongue again in a sort of seductive growl. "What a pretty name."

She blushes and then looks down at her lap. "I like the way you say that," she whispers, right before she laughs nervously, and then looks back up with another bashful grin. "My name."

Oh, Sandra, you're making this entirely too easy.

Leaning against her desk, feet crossed at the ankles, I fold my arms over my chest and bite my bottom lip as I take her in. She grins with excitement right before she bashfully looks away, but not before her eyes graze down my frame, stopping when they reach my cock.

So scandalous, Sandy. What would all the little boys think?

"Do you think you can make an exception, just this once?" I ask, a sort of tempting seduction dripping from my lips as I study her and wait for her to tell me yes.

Because we both know she will. She goes to rebuttal. Most likely about to object.

Stop with the fucking games, Sandra.

But I cut her off quickly, and say, "If you can, I'd like to take you out to dinner, Sandy. That is, if your boyfriend won't mind?"

"I... I... don't have a boyfriend," she stammers, her same anxious chuckle from before filling the space between us a moment later.

"Husband?" I ask, playing right along, although she's arguably too young to have one of those. Then again, in the world of Botox, plastic surgery, and boob jobs, who the fuck knows anymore. Her blush deepens as she smiles and looks back down at her lap.

Eyes up here, Sandra.

Confidence is sexy. Bashful and inexperienced is not.

"You ever been with a man, Sandy?"

Her eyes bolt up to meet mine, shocked, horrified, and slightly fucking turned on, there's no denying it.

"On a date. Out to dinner?" I deadpan, earning me a nervous swallow from the girl sitting across from me as I grin with mischief.

She looks around my back, taking her time, assessing her options, and wondering how best to respond. "I guess, just this once," she finally whispers.

She reaches over and grabs a card off the left corner of her desk. Leaning forward, I capture her wrist and pull her into me, noticing the gasp as it escapes her lips and the tremble in her arm as I lean in even closer the same second I slide the card from her grasp and hold it behind my back.

"Sandy," I breathe, as I stand and keep her eyes locked on my own. Her face is so close I can almost taste her innocence as the card slips from my fingers and into the hands of Magnolia. "On second thought, maybe you shouldn't let me take you out."

I hear the click of the lock behind her as Magnolia unlocks the door, but Sandy is too far gone to notice and only stares desperately into my eyes.

Game fucking won.

"Why?" she desperately breathes, just as Magnolia slips the key back in my hand before disappearing through the door.

"Because," I smile, as I back away and close my hand over the key. "Men like me have an appetite you're not used to. A craving you've never seen before." Her eyes fill slightly with fear as I unlock the door Magnolia just passed through. "Trust me, it's a hunger that serves only to scare you." My purpose here served, I toss the key back at her startled expression and wink. "And entirely nothing you'd ever have the skill to handle, little one."

I make my exit before she can reply and I'm immediately met with the angry eyes of Magnolia as we start to make our way down the hall.

"Appetites, cravings, hunger?" she asks annoyed. "Really, Dec, a schoolgirl would have the skill you'd require with crappy ass lines like that."

We move quickly, strategically, aware of our surroundings, and ready for anything that might prevent us from getting what we came here for. I sit with her comment a moment, irritated and contemplating how best to respond just as Timmy emerges from the door at the end of the corridor, limping slightly from the wound in his leg and smiling ear to ear like a kid on Christmas morning.

Fucking Timmy, horrible timing as always.

Stopping abruptly, I square off against Magnolia as we wait for our accomplice to get his ass over here and hopefully tell us "mission accomplished."

"Mm, schoolgirl," I groan as she stops beside me. "You're giving me ideas, Mags. Is that an invitation to 'school' you on the skills required to quench my thirst? Or is this just the student cock-teasing the professor like usual? Because it's been a long time, Sweetheart, but I can guarantee you, I'd find the greatest pleasure in being your tutor. Bringing you up to speed quickly. Reminding you what you've been missing over the past seven years."

"Over my dead body," she fumes, but I see the lust building in her eyes. Feel the temptation building between us because fucking my wife, good and hard like we both like it, has always been both of our weaknesses.

"Necrophilia isn't my thing, Magnolia," I hiss back with irritation, needing her to break so I can claim her and take her back as my own. She's the damn lifeline I've been living too long without. "I prefer my women warm, wet, and willing."

"Classic," she retorts, her eyes glancing up and down my body with growing need. "The irony is, I find it hard to believe you've ever found a woman who was truly willing."

"Present company excluded?"

"Fuck off, Dec!"

"Only if you're the one doing the fucking."

"I got it!" Timmy shouts as he hobbles over to us and finally meets us in the middle of the hallway. His enthusiasm makes both Magnolia and I glance over our shoulders and hurry him towards the nearest exit. Obviously not the one Sandy monitors. I'm certainly not as irrational as Magnolia seems to think.

"Good work, Timothy," Magnolia praises him as we make it back out into the black of night. I roll my eyes as the nerd smiles like his mother just patted him on the back. She takes the zip drive from his hand and pockets it quickly. "Now, let's take it back to the house and make sure it's got everything we need on it."

"And if it doesn't?" Our little friend questions. I take note and watch as he begins to worry with each step that takes him back into his own personal hell.

My hand quickly finds his shoulder and I grip hard, watching as the dork slightly jumps out of his pathetic skin. "Then we'll deal with it, Tim. The only way we know how."

His fearful shudder isn't lost on me as we reach the car and I force him into the back seat. My eyes quickly raise and catch her blue ones over the hood. The look she gives me forces us both to a stop as we finally realize the only way out of the hell we've created between us is to force ourselves painfully through it.

Destroy our never ending purgatory. And just pray it doesn't gut us in the process.

We'll deal with it alright.

Right after I deal with Magnolia.

7

TUESDAY

11:45 P.M.

THE DARK SIDE of truth is we all try to deny what we're all hiding. The one thing that likely has the power to destroy us. We believe we're preserving our honor when what's really happening is our own self-sabotage. We stumble around blindly into a sort of disloyal treason, twisted by the idea that we're covering up our secret perfectly.

My crime is no different.

"The signal is weak, but it's there," Magnolia says as she leans into the monitors and presses a button.

We're in my office, strategically attached to my bedroom, and the wall of screens in front of us comes to life as pictures of the capital of China and Russia quickly come into view. Scattered throughout the feed is video surveillance from the country's military headquarters. My hand slips into my pockets as I study each video and subconsciously roll around the gold band I keep hidden there between my fingers. A bad habit I can't break, and one I never intend to, either.

"Looks like Timmy came through after all," I admit. "You want to give him the good news he's in the clear, or should I?"

Magnolia clicks a few more buttons and changes the feed. A spetsnaz, from the Russian federation, walks across the screen and I study him closely, aware that I still haven't told Magnolia why we used our little friend to gain access to the Russian satellites. But if I know her like I think I do, she's onto my secret. I just hope she keeps her lips sealed long enough for me to get us the justice we both deserve.

"Let's make him sweat," she says mischievously. "A few more hours under close surveillance won't hurt him. Hell, it'll probably be good for him once they find out what he's done."

She has a point. The last time we used an inside man to accomplish a job we couldn't, he never made it home. Rumors surfaced, and most hold no merit, like rumors often don't. But, if I had to guess the closest to the truth, I'd say his body was dismembered slowly, inch by inch, and shipped off to the country who believed hired him to do their dirty work. In the end, it was more blood spilled that I'm responsible for, even when I never pulled a damn trigger.

"Careful, Dec," Magnolia whispers as she eases away from the monitors and studies me closely from across the room. "Your weakness is showing."

Burying my thoughts for the moment, I cock my head to the side and glare at her. "Now what would you know about my weakness, Sweetheart?"

"Your one flaw is easy to see," she suggests with bitterness on her tongue as she crosses one arm over the other. "The slip in your otherwise always perfectly orchestrated control gives you away. The fact that you won't be able to stop whatever happens to him once he's released. It kind of hits a sore spot, doesn't it?

Maybe even makes you think of the one thing you try to keep hidden in the past."

"It's hard to keep the past hidden when it's constantly staring me in the face, Magnolia."

"Me?" she fakes innocence.

"Who else? Unless you want to lie to me and tell me you've forgotten?" She stares at me as loathing fills her beautiful eyes but she doesn't answer. When she still hasn't spoken after a moment, I laugh and say, "don't tell me you've grown that heartless after all this time?"

"Heartless!" she yells, her face flushing red with rage. "Fuck it! You know what, Ace? I guess I am, seeing that my heart was forever ripped away from me that night!"

"And mine wasn't?"

"You were supposed to protect them!" She screams. "You were supposed to lay down your life for them, like I would've mine!"

"Who's to say I didn't!"

"I am!" She yells as she storms towards me and pushes against my chest. "How can you call yourself a man, Declan? How can you continue to let yourself live when you let them die? How can you stand to look at me every single day and not remember..."

I take a step into her and cut her off, fueled with a new kind of madness and done with all the bullshit.

This stops now. That hatred. The lies. The constant blame for a fate we can't go back and change.

"All I do is relive it, Magnolia," I seethe as I grab her hands and attempt to stop her from beating my chest. "All I do is regret. Attempt to fucking repent for my sins that night made me guilty of. I silently grieve, every damn day, and wish I could take it away. Wish I could change it. For you. Even if it kills me in the process, Sweetheart."

Her eyes cloud over with darkness as she glares at me, disbelieving every word I just said. Her breathing turns ragged, enraged, as her hand slips from my grip and I realize my mistake a little too late.

"Well," she whispers, as her hand raises, and I catch the glimmer of metal in the corner of my eye. "Then maybe I can help you out with that."

Before I can blink, she has a knife held to my throat. The blade pierces my skin as her eyes glass over with tears. Fuck it. If this is the way it needs to be, so be it. I harshly take another step forward, feeling the warm trickle of blood down my neck as her hand begins to shake in desperation.

"Go ahead," I growl. "Do it, Mags. I know you've been fantasizing about it for fucking years."

Her eyes grow wide as she glances down at the knife and her hands begin to tremble a little more. A tear falls down her cheek as she looks back up, her horror flashing through her eyes as she remembers all that took place seven years ago. Everything we can't get back. Everything we felt for each other then flares in her deep blue eyes as she holds my life in her hands.

"I welcome death, Magnolia," I hiss, as I lean in, and the blade presses further into my throat. "Every fucking day. I live to die. To be put out of my misery. To not feel any more pain. But, do you want to know the sickest truth of all, Sweetheart? Even if I felt all the suffering in the world as you slowly pulled that knife across my neck, it wouldn't even come close to the torment I'm forced to walk through daily knowing, yes, I could've stopped it. Fuck, Magnolia, I could've saved them."

Fresh tears fall down her face as she presses the cold metal harder into my throat. "You're already in hell, Declan," she hisses, finally understanding what I've been trying to show her. "Glad I could be the one to put you there."

She backs away as her hand lowers, defeated by the memories we both try so hard to suppress. I grab the knife quickly, spinning her around and capturing her tightly around the waist. Her gasp mixes with her tears as I raise her knife to her delicate skin, right below her ear and the curve of her chin, then slowly press in.

"Hell, Sweetheart?" I taunt, a sinister laugh escaping my lips. "Hell is too kind a word for how I feel having to look at you every single day, and not have you like I did before."

"You never had me, Ace."

I run the tip of the knife slowly down and then back up her neck, pressing in only when I feel her defiance grow. She stills in my arms, her breaths quickening.

"Keep fucking with my head, Magnolia, like I want to fuck your body, and you'll see just how much I'll have you," I growl in her ear. "Any way I'd like. I'll fucking have you."

"I thought you wanted willing," she anxiously whispers. "Holding a knife to my neck should prove I'll never consent."

A normal man might take her at her words, but I've been trained to always stay alert to my surroundings. I'm skilled in the art of deception, and I notice her betrayal as her hips subconsciously grind back into my crotch. Her desire's evident in that small gesture, her hidden consent, suddenly given to me, making me only want to push us further. Make us finally fall over our damned edge.

"Agree to disagree," my menacing chuckle feathers softly across her neck as I press against her ass and my grip on her waist tightens. Her skin prickles, a small shiver runs deliciously down her spine, only proving as more silent evidence of her permission, and fuck, I plan on wasting no time claiming it.

I hook her hands behind her back and clasp them together as she tries to break free. Dropping the knife to the floor in the process, I kick it under the desk quickly and then focus back on Magnolia. Her head thrashes from side to side in protest as her lips spew insults and she pushes back against my frame, but I'm finally game to call her on all her fucking bullshit as I sink my mouth down against her neck, and attempt to stop her defiance. I smile when she grows silent and stills in my arms. Her addictive moan of pleasure fills the room a second later as my mouth works with heated purpose, sucking its way up to her ear in earnest, deliberate force. Feeling around on the desk behind me, I grab a pair of handcuffs and secure her while she's perfectly distracted.

"Restraining the victim only proves my point," she moans louder as I tighten the metal around her wrist and press my hardening cock into her ass.

"What point is that exactly, Sweetheart," I growl as I prove *my point* by grinding my hardening length against her, groaning out in pleasure myself as I feel it slip between her firm ass cheeks. "How you like to fuck with me? Or the consent you're failing to hide when we both know you're more than willing?"

Swinging her around, her mouth falls open in shock and I lean in swiftly, taking her bottom lip between my teeth. My hands skate down the sides of her frame, pulling her closer and securing her against my chest as I slowly lick her lips, coaxing them open as her breaths come in short lust-filled pants against my own. Lifting my right hand, I push her hair off the side of her neck, only releasing her soft lips when I feel her body finally start to submit, and then stare deeply into her eyes.

"Don't do this," she begs, but her eyes tell me a different story. One she's been hiding. One she's pleading with me to see through now, and hell, as I stand there with her in my arms, I wonder why it's taken me this long to notice.

Crushing my mouth against hers, I step forward, pushing her back into the next room. She attempts to fight me with her kiss. She's angry. Together we're unhinged. The way her mouth moves against mine in harsh desire makes turning back now definitely not an option. It only fuels me. Our teeth clash, tongues deliriously tangle, as I fist her hair in my hand and force her to continue stepping backward until her thighs hit the bed.

"Keep going, Ace, I dare you," she purrs as our mouths break apart and I plunge the top of her dress down around her small waist, quickly taking her right perk nipple in between my lips. She moans, eagerly waiting for me to do the same with her other tit. "I warned you once, remember?" she breathlessly whispers, as I oblige and take her left nipple in my hot mouth. "I'd still enjoy every second of destroying your manhood. *Bit. By little bit.*"

I grab her hips and pull them against mine so she can feel just how hard I am, *how little I'm not*, as my tongue flicks against her nipple. I smile against her breasts when her shocked gasp fills my ears and then attempt to pull her even closer against me, because damn it, I can't get her close enough.

"Are you going to shut that disrespectful mouth, Sweetheart?" I groan, as my hands roam her body with greed. "Or am I going to have to shut it for you?"

Raising her skirt, I feel my way around to her perfect ass. Forcing her center against my throbbing length, my fingers dip lower, under the fabric of her panties and I groan when I find her dripping with her *consent*. She complies perfectly, bending to my demands after seven damn years, as her hips grind against my straining cock.

God, I've missed this.

Fuck kryptonite, Magnolia is both my life and my impending death. A hurricane filled with the power to destroy me. She's right about one thing. I'm a damn fool who'll always walk through her relentless hell if it meant getting a taste of her breathtaking heaven.

"Contempt is the only thing you'll ever hear from me," she whispers, but we both know it's a lie. A lie I'm determined to break, starting with her hot mouth that has constantly proved it needs to be disciplined.

Tracing my fingers along the seam of her panties, our needy moans escalate, filling the room when I feel her drenched need coating her velvet lips. Pressing into her soft opening, her wetness grows and drips down my fingers as I pull her panties to the side and pull one finger across her seam.

"So eager," I whisper, as I reluctantly release her body and give her a push against the mattress. I raise my hand to my lips, sucking her *consent* from my fingertips before starting to untie my tie. "In your contempt, you neglect to hide your enjoyment, Sweetheart," I smile as I nod down at her drenched thighs. "Your soaking wet pussy is begging for me to touch it. Not that I can blame her. It's been a long time since she's been ravaged, fucking possessed, claimed, only the way I know how."

She looks up at me with hatred for the way her body betrays her, and fuck, it just makes my dick harder. Pulling my tie from my neck, I climb up her frame, wrapping my left arm around her waist and hoisting her up towards the headboard. She lets down her guard and gives herself to me a little more as she sighs with satisfaction. Another sure giveaway that she wants, fuck that, needs, what she's been denying us both for far too long.

Looking down, I admire my handiwork. Arms clasped behind her back. Breasts exposed, nipples hard. Her dress pulled up around her waist and her panties torn to the side exposing her wet, velvet lips. My gaze drifts across every inch of skin I've missed touching. Every freckle. Every blemish that makes her so much more perfect in my eyes and my heart breaks inside. But it's when my gaze lifts and locks with her own that my damned heart bursts. It hits me. It's in this moment I can finally see what I've been searching for reflected in her eyes. The words that I've been begging to hear her say for seven years.

That it wasn't my fault. That she forgives me. That she'll never be anyone else's but mine.

Grabbing the top of her dress, I rip it down the middle in one swift motion causing her back to arch and her head to fall back in need as a thrilling cry escapes her lips. Anxiously finding the buckle of my belt, I start to unclasp it from my waist when her head falls forward and her eyes cloud over. What I saw moments ago was a minor slip in her otherwise impenetrable armor, and she's not done running that mouth of hers yet tonight.

"You think I enjoy this?" She breathes heavily. "Watching you take the part of me that's easiest to covet? My body. Your aim's gotten sloppy over the years, Ace. Maybe if you tried a little harder next time, you'd actually get what you really wanted. My mind. My heart. And not just what's easiest for you to take."

I fling the belt from my slacks instantly and roll it over my fist a few times. Leaning in, we war with each other as our glares deepen and for just a brief moment, I swear I see surrender in her eyes. Reaching behind her, I grab her wrists, unlocking her cuffs, and then pull them above her head. Looping my belt around her wrists, I lock them together tightly before attaching her to the headboard, and make sure she's more than secure. I give her just enough room to move around, and smile as I watch her writhe under me in pleasure, in hostility, in desire. Watching her tantalizing show only makes me want to give her what we've both been denying we want.

Our union.

"Looks like you can't keep that hot little mouth shut, can you?" I grin, rising off the bed and then watching as her eyes widen. It hasn't been that long since I owned her body and soul, and she knows what kind of punishment for her sins is going to happen next. "Let me help you with that, Magnolia."

I smile as her face pales and her knees fall together in a slight protest. I can't help but chuckle at the sight, knowing they'll open for me wider than they ever have before, even if I have to pry them apart and keep them there.

Walking to my dresser across the room, I open the top drawer and smile knowing how much we're both going to enjoy this. Removing her only option, I turn and make my way back, delighting when I see her body rise in need.

"You wouldn't dare," she warns only to have her hips tilt up craving what she's earned.

Straddling her hips, I place the gag against her mouth and force her lips open, wider, wider, stretching her lips until the ball fits securely in her hot little mouth. She eyes me wildly as I fasten it behind her head and feel her body tense beautifully beneath me.

"Magnolia," I sigh, as I slowly lower myself down her frame. "It was the only way for us both to enjoy this."

Pushing her legs apart, my face falls to the inside of her thigh as I lick up her slick skin, finally breathing in the pussy I can't wait to feast on after all this time. In a sexual haze, I glance up into her eyes and see them cloud over. She's hungry, ravenous, needing a release she hasn't had in far too long.

"Don't fucking look away," I growl as her eyes widen and I lean closer into her scent. "I want to watch you take this. I want to see all your pleasure, and the unrelenting pain it causes you to give me your repentance. You're mine, Sweetheart. Always have been. Always will be. Now, let me remind you what it feels like to be owned by a fucking King."

Holding her gaze, I slowly lick up her seam and hear her muffled moans of pleasure before I stick my tongue deep inside her walls. Fuck, she does taste like the perfect mixture of heaven and hell, and as I suck my way up to her clit, enter two fingers inside her tight cunt and never take my eyes off her own, I silently make us a promise as she begins to grind her hips against my face.

I'll never let the way we feel in this moment slip away from us ever again.

Together, we're fucking perfect.

Complete. Finally whole.

Euphoric in this moment, with a love we haven't felt in far too long.

8

WEDNESDAY

12:30 A.M.

HER MUFFLED screams attempt to rip through the room, muted by her punishment, the gag in her mouth. Magnolia convulses under me in a continuous wave of ecstasy, a hurricane of sweet pleasure as her storm hits my tongue and I groan in satisfaction as I drink her all up. My eyes raise and watch as her hips surge, her head falls back in an all-encompassing pleasure, and then her center grinds back down against my mouth as her head snaps forward and her eyes lock with my own.

Before I let her body come down completely, I release her sex and crawl up her frame. Unfastening her gag, I quickly throw it to the side and crush my lips against hers as she sucks my tongue into her mouth, greedy, hungry to taste just how much I made her feel alive after all this time. Tearing my shirt from my body, I release her mouth only for a second to pull it over my head.

"Your cock," she pants. "I need it. Now. Don't make me ask again."

Smiling, I stand and slip out of my shoes before pushing my slacks and briefs to the floor. Climbing back on the bed, I stroke her sensitive clit and whisper, "Where?"

But before I can coax an answer out of her, she claims my mouth again and kisses me so fiercely I can't force myself to release her and stop. Her teeth claim my bottom lip as I raise over her body and press my tip against her entrance. She bucks under me and purrs into my mouth as I suck her tongue between my lips. She needs me to fill her. Wants me to thrust inside her and give her what she craves most.

Our own, selfish, atonement.

"Tell me you've missed this, Magnolia," I growl as her wetness covers the crown of my pulsing dick. "Tell me you've wanted this, just as much as I've needed it, Sweetheart."

I back away from her slightly and run my fingers up the inside of her thigh, quickly sticking one, then two inside her. Her hips raise, inviting me in, and I spread her moisture backward, pressing lightly into her tight ass. She gasps as I suck her tongue into my mouth once again and groan. She's so tight. I can't help myself and find I press into her ass further as her hips raise in wanting and precum drips out of my cock telling me only one thing - we both want more. I look down between us and grab my length, expressing as much as I can from the crown and then glance back up and see her eyes cloud over with lust.

"Open," I demand, feeling my cock twitch when she obliges.

Swiping my cum across her lips, I watch as her tongue darts out, her eyes close and she purrs, content, and delighted with my taste in her hot mouth. "Good girl," I hiss before claiming her mouth with my own and getting drunk on her taste mixed with my own as it delectably swirls around our tongues. Mixed together, we're a dangerous concoction, making us both delirious and desperately in need of another fix.

Reaching up, I untie her from the headboard and then wrap my arm around her waist. Flipping her on her stomach in one swift move, I refasten her hands to the headboard, binding them tightly together. She gasps, but the sound is quickly cut off as I slap her pale ass and then groan when I see it blush from my own kind of self-seeking retribution. Grabbing her red cheek, I massage it for a moment and look down, mesmerized by the view of her wet pussy and tight ass, and entirely still unbelieving that she's in my bed, surrendering to me after all this time.

"More," she moans with need. I smile, happy to give her what she requests, as her hips tilt and she angles her pussy up, giving me every man's most treasured view.

"Your body needs me to release it," I whisper as I lean down and lick from her clit all the way back across her ass. She gasps before a shocked sigh leaves her lips, making my balls tighten with the need for my own release. "Tell me you need me to set you free, Mags," I say as I pull two fingers through her slick folds. "Tell me," I whisper further, as I lean in and stick them inside her pussy. "You need me to set *us* free." She stills, and it takes all my power to not break and stop with her as I pull my fingers through her growing wetness, spreading it back further across her ass. "Tell me, Sweetheart, that you need me to make you cum."

"Yes," she consents instantly, more eager than I could have hoped for. I drop between her thighs, the same thirsty need rushing through me. I'm driven by only one desire, to feel her explode against my lips once again.

Rolling onto my back, I crawl between her legs and lick up her heat. She complies perfectly, riding my face faster than she ever did before as her scent drags me under, her taste pushes me into a frenzy, and I bite down lightly on her clit, hearing her slight scream, before sucking it between my lips.

"More," she pants from above as I force her legs apart and

look up into her eyes, making her watch as she rides my face and I suck her pussy lips into my mouth.

Her stare clouds over with a darker desire than I've ever witnessed before as my tongue parts her folds with strong intention and her wetness grows. Sticking a finger inside her pussy, I suck down hard on her bud as I reach behind her and stick another finger in her ass. She screams out as her head falls back and it only takes a few seconds for her second orgasm to rip through her. I let her ride it out this time, her hips thrashing against my mouth as she cries, screams, explodes with such force against my mouth I almost can't keep up as I drink her down, slowly pulling my finger out of her tight ass before licking up what's left of her pleasure. She looks thoroughly satisfied as she glances down between her legs at me. I grin before gently placing a kiss against her velvet lips, grabbing her ass in my hands, and stopping her movements for a brief moment and taking the time to enjoy us finally together like this.

We stare into each other's eyes, our breaths labored and coming in quick lustful pants filled with the deepest pleasure. So many things are still left unsaid, and there's still so much we need to discuss. But fuck, we've always had a way of talking that's better than any words we could ever exchange. As I grip her hips in my hands and stare in her eyes, I know we're both finally on the same page.

Slipping out from underneath her, I climb off the bed and watch her eye me over her shoulder. "Still want more, Magnolia?"

She doesn't respond, only tries to catch her breath as I reach under the bed frame and pull out her next reward. Her hot mouth has told me off one too many times over the past seven years. It's time she remembers what happens when she runs it and refuses to stop.

"You never told me where you want my cock," I tease, as her eyes widen, and I grab one of her legs before she can stop me. Attaching her ankle to the long black bar, I spread her legs wide and do the same to her other ankle as I climb back on the bed. She gasps as I reach underneath her and pull her waist up, her ass cheeks parting beautifully, and I take no time in rubbing my length slowly between them. She groans into the sheets before glancing back over her shoulder and locking eyes with me once again. "Should I put it where I want?" I taunt, but she doesn't answer.

I spread her cheeks out further, watching and delighting in the fact that her legs are bound by the bar, stretched out as far as they will go. Her tight hole puckering in need when I line my dick up against it. She cries out the second I breach her hole; hot tears prick her eyes. I watch her for any sign that she doesn't want this, that this isn't part of her consent, as I hold only the tip inside her ass. "Fuck, you're so tight," I growl as her mouth opens and she gets lost in the forbidden pleasure. "Your ass forgot how to take my cock, Sweetheart."

I rotate my length around in circles, slowly working in, gathering her wetness from her pussy and spreading it backwards while I watch her eyes for any sign she's unwilling. But fuck, she wants this. I can see it. I can feel it. What's more, I know it. I press in further only when I know she's ready.

"You never told me where," I growl with the best fucking pleasure I've felt in seven damn years as I give her one last chance to change her mind. "Should I stop? Or fuck your tight asshole like I want?"

She says nothing, only stares back in my eyes, aroused, drugged by my control, letting me decide for both of us. "I always knew you liked it dirty, Sweetheart," I whisper when I can't hold back any longer. "Hold on, Magnolia, because I'm not stopping until we're both fucking screaming."

Thrusting inside her, she screams out my name just as I reach around and spank her throbbing clit. Rubbing it in circles and groaning out against her back as I pull out of her ass and thrust back inside it again, she cries out my name and tells me not to stop. Harder, faster, determined to get what I want and give her what she fucking needs, I pinch her bud hard between my fingers, then slap it stronger than before as I pound into her ass from behind, relentless, atoning for both our sins, as she cries out against the sheets.

"Fuck, I love how you take it," I groan, thrusting into her and showing no signs of slowing down. "Your body was made for me."

"Declan," she whimpers, as I reluctantly slow and feel her body nearing her third release. "Please, I don't think I can..."

She crashes over the edge a second later as I rub her clit, coaxing another release from her tight body. I slowly pull in and out of her ass as my fingers dip into her pulsing pussy, deliberate, gradual, in no rush and wanting her to feel every perfectly numbing moment of her climax before I pull my fingers back up to her clit. The motion makes her orgasm start all over again as she screams my name and fists the headboard in her handcuffed grasp.

"That's right, Sweetheart," I whisper, as I roll her bud under my fingers, slide my dick from her ass, and then kiss down her spine before lowering myself between her legs. "I think I've finally gone and fucked the fight out of you, Magnolia."

She gasps for air as I remove my fingertips from her clit, unbuckle her ankles, remove the bar, and then start to unclasp her wrists. A tear falls down her cheek as I pull the belt from the headboard, and quickly gather her in my arms.

"More," she softly cries against my neck, and fuck, I can't help but feel the burn of my own tears in my throat as my heart grabs ahold of her surrendering plea.

"I'll always give you more," I whisper, gently laying her back on the mattress. Her legs eagerly part, and my length slides tenderly this time inside her slick walls. When we're finally joined, my cock pushing deep inside her and forcing her pussy to its max, I still and force her to look me in the eyes so she hears each and every damn word I say next. "Always. Forever. For eternity, Sweetheart. As long as you want me, Magnolia, you'll have me."

"I've always wanted you, Dec," she whimpers, a hushed confession that startles us both as her body begins to shake, her bottom lip trembles, and I lean my forehead against hers and gently start to move my hips.

"I know," I confess for the both of us, knowing we're both at a loss for words after all this time.

Her mouth finds mine, but for the first time in seven years, her bite means no harm. Our lips part as our eyes stay locked, our bodies become one, and our souls connect for the first time since *it* happened. We draw out the moment, lazy, content, finally agreeing to a truce as our bodies move in harmony and our lips devour a new beginning breaking free on our tongues. One I know we never thought was possible.

"I've missed you, Ace," she whispers on a desperate cry as I pick up the pace. My thrusts become demanding, her body begins to tighten, and she fiercely starts to chase another climax. "I've wanted you, just like this, as much as you needed and wanted me, too."

"I know," I smile as I capture her lips against mine. Our truce, finally agreed upon for now, as we both cry out in earth shattering ecstasy a few minutes later.

9

WEDNESDAY

3 A.M.

THE PAST only serves one purpose.

To destroy you if you let it.

We struggle for power from the day we're born.

We wrestle with control from inception.

From the second we take our first breath; we feel both invincible and paralyzed by the fact that we're fucking mortal.

Most days we can convince ourselves that the lie we've built is impenetrable. Bulletproof to all the fiction we've surrounded ourselves with. An illusion that only seeks to destroy us.

I'm no exception if I don't play my cards right.

But, my most honest truth is, I'd give up all power, all control, if it meant I could change our past. Magnolia and my own. Erase the nightmare that haunts us daily. But the truth is, we both can't outrun it, no matter how much bullshit we try to throw at one another along the way.

As I hold Magnolia in my arms, feel her heavy breaths feather across my chest, and subconsciously pull her tighter against me, I know no matter how many lies we've tricked ourselves into believing, we're sentenced to be forever ruined. Gutted. Shattered by the fact that if we don't face our past head on, it'll always get the better of us.

"Do you miss them?" she whispers, and my breathing stops. I will my hands not to shake, but they tremble slightly as they run up and down the length of her spine. I sit in agonizing silence for a moment and roll her question around in my mind.

Do I miss them? She can't be serious. Of course, I fucking miss them.

"Every second," I grit out through clenched teeth. "Every day. Every powerless moment I'm forced to realize my worst mistake. That I failed them. I failed us."

She sighs and pulls me in closer. Her voice shaking as she replies, "Every night. Every morning. Every time I look in your eyes. My biggest fear is that I'll one day forget them, Dec. If I do what I know is right in order for me to heal. Let you go."

"Never," I demand harshly, a possessive jealousy coursing through my veins as my grip on her tightens. "You'll never forget. I won't let you. What's more, you can *forget* the idea of ever letting me go. That concept is inconsequential now, don't you think? Time, and the way I fucked you into submission moments ago, should be proof enough."

"Mm," she seductively sighs as she pulls me closer. "Kind of like the way my mouth fucks you into submission, outside the bedroom, Ace."

I laugh wholeheartedly, "Yeah, Sweetheart," I smile. "Kind of like that."

We both fall silent, wrapped in each other's arms, and enjoying the brief lighthearted feeling between us for the first time in years. But it doesn't last long.

"That's what scares me most," she startles, being pulled back into our past and having a one-track mind I can't seem to break through, no matter how hard I try. "I don't want to remember, and I don't want to forget. But how can I do either when I can't stand to be near you, and can't live without you, Declan?"

My heavy sigh echoes through the room as I reluctantly release my hold on her. I sit up on my side, letting her slip from my arms and feeling the coldness seep in between us. Sternly looking her in her eyes, I get lost for a moment in everything that encompasses us. The past. The present. The fucked-up nightmare we'll never be able to forget.

How can I answer her?

We're cursed.

I know it as surely as I'm sitting here about to take my next breath. Over time, I've just found a way to deny it. What I've grown to realize is, my *wife, Magnolia,* can't.

"If I knew I was going to lose you," I whisper, reaching out and brushing a strand of hair out of her eyes. "I would've killed myself when I had the courage. When the pain was so strong, I was delirious and mad trying to stop it."

"Don't," my wife whispers as she takes my hand and pulls me closer. "Don't make false promises in hindsight that you don't have the guts now to fulfill," she teases with a small smile, but I see the depths of her despair crying out in her eyes. A tormenting storm staring at me from deep inside her soul. I look down at our joined hands and find myself strangled by the truth we both don't want to face. The fact that even if we forgive each other, even if we try and move on from our tragedy, we'll never, ever, be able to forget it.

"I mean it Magnolia," I insist as I look back up and silently beg her to not look away. Facing the past is hard, but it's impossible not to look at when she stares back in my eyes. "Losing our children was the death of me. The only thing that kept me alive since then, was knowing you were still breathing. That you were still somewhere in this world with me. Even if you wouldn't have me in your bed, and even if you didn't want me to be a part of your life. Knowing that you never filed for divorce gave me hope, when I damn sure didn't deserve it. It made me believe we had a chance, when I should've never been given the smallest possibility of your future. If you had really left me, filed for divorce, that for sure would've killed me, even when loosing them didn't."

She looks down between us, averting her eyes from mine this time and hiding her thoughts. My chest hurts with a soul sucking pain I haven't felt in years as I study her, waiting to see how she'll respond to my confession. Right now, I want only one thing. To show her that what we had can be brought back to life. If we're both willing.

"Why did you," I question before I can think better of it. "Why did you not let me murder myself when you had the chance? Why'd you never ask for a divorce? Because I'm going to be honest, Sweetheart. I don't think I would've been so nice if the tables were turned."

"Because," she looks up suddenly, answering without pause as she bites her bottom lip. "Because, I *knew* that would've ended you. I knew that would've pushed you over the edge. I lost my children, Dec. *Our children.* I couldn't lose the only other part of my soul I had left. My last reason for breathing. You, Ace."

I'm stunned, speechless, wrecked as my mind races and I take in all she has just said. She falls silent for a moment, the quiet stretching between us like a ticking bomb, threatening to explode worse than ever before if we both don't silence our pride and say what needs to be said.

What's in our hearts.

When she doesn't continue after a while, I go to speak but she quickly cuts me off before I can get the chance. "Even if living beside you these past seven years has made me walk through hell on earth, Dec, and even if," she whispers as tears prick her eyes, "walking beside you, has made me wish they took me instead."

"Mags, I..." but my words fail me as I fall speechless and get lost in her tearful stare. Instead, I pull her close and nestle her head under my chin, not able to look her in the eyes any longer. Having her here with me, like this, is more than I ever wished or ever could've asked for.

"You want to know the saddest part?" I ask as she buries her face against my chest. "I tried."

She doesn't say a word. Silence stretches once again between us, and I can tell she's struggling to understand.

"I tried to kill myself, Magnolia." Her body tenses in my arms, she goes to speak, but I pull her closer and stop her before she can cut me off again. "A week, maybe two after they were gone. But I couldn't. I failed. Just like I failed us that night. I wanted nothing more than to not live anymore. To not breathe in a world without them. But how can I leave this world and enter a whole new hell without you in it, Sweetheart? I couldn't leave you. Not even for them. But fuck, Magnolia, I want you to know I tried."

"I don't blame you, Dec. For anything," my heart bursts at her words as my throat tightens. After all this time, I can't believe my ears as she tells me everything I've needed to hear. "Truth be told. It took every amount of courage I had not to want to end myself."

"'I'd feel better if you did," I whisper, feeling a void from the release of my self-inflicting penance after all this time. "Blame me."

"Masochist," she laughs, attempting to lighten the mood.

"Sweetheart," I growl, as I lift her thigh and pull her naked form up against my side. "You have no idea!"

She smiles against my chest and let myself get lost in this tiny moment of bliss between us. A moment when we're both bared to each other, body and soul. When there is nothing left unsaid between us. When the past isn't holding us back and we can pretend we love each other like we used to. *Once upon a beautiful time,* before our son and daughter were taken from us, held for ransom, beaten and then brutally murdered to prove a sick point. A sick message, that we're never in as much control as we think we are. The silence between us stretches, serving as an admission of surrender, if only for this brief moment. And I take it, relish in it, drown in the fact that for maybe only this one-second, in our fucked-up *once upon a time*, we've both won.

But time does what it does best in our blissful exchange, it passes.

"So, what do we do now," she sighs.

Fuck if I know, because I can't promise her she won't look in my eyes when the sun rises and not want to kill me tomorrow when our past becomes too heavy a weight to carry. I also can't guarantee that I won't want to rip her clothes off and force her to remember how good we could still be, if she'd only let me back in after that inevitably happens.

It's a sick dance we waltz around ever since our life ended seven years ago. A morbid tango, as she sways me one way and I try to swing her around to the other.

"Well," I sigh, as my palm falls to her ass, and I give it a tight squeeze, pulling her harder against my side. "We still need to cut our little friend, Timmy, loose. I'm sure he's sweated under enough pressure for one lifetime, don't you think."

"Or?" she suggests, mischief hanging in her tone that makes my balls tighten and my dick start to harden.

"Or," I hiss, as I pull her up to straddle my hips, then groan in pleasure when she rocks her wet cunt against my thick length. "You can tell me to go to hell and I can fuck your sassy mouth into submission again. Your call, Sweetheart. But just so we're clear, my preference is the latter."

"Is that so, Ace," she smiles as her face drops towards mine.

Her mouth parts and she licks my bottom lip before sucking it into her mouth. Any restraint I have left snaps as I grab her hips possessively and tempt her to rock them against my now throbbing dick. She obliges, flawlessly, as she raises her hips, grabs my thick cock in her small hand and slides her wet sex slowly down, taking me completely inside her.

"Fucking hell, Magnolia," I hiss, as she lifts and then thrusts down with enough greed in her slick heat to make me want to blow my load inside her right now. She moves fast. Hungry. Selfishly. Over and over again as my mouth falls open and I watch her through a thick haze, mesmerized by how sexy she looks riding my cock.

"Hell, Ace?" she asks, but I almost don't hear her as my mind clouds, our bodies slap together, my fingers dig harshly into her hips and we both cry out from the feeling of my thick cock buried deep inside her. "Is that what this is?"

"Fuck! If this is hell, I would've gladly killed myself seven-years ago."

Her movements stop as she takes in what I just said, her eyes clouding over with fresh tears. Something snaps inside me, a desire to keep us here, where the weight of all we're forced to carry is lighter. Not dragged back down into the past that'll end us the longer we stay there. Reaching behind her, I slap her ass hard and hiss out as she screams, her pussy tightens, and she braces her hands against my chest.

"You want to know what happens *now*," I growl. "You ride my fucking cock like the damn queen we both know you are. I'll tell you when you can fucking stop."

10

WEDNESDAY

5 A.M.

OUR TWISTED PAST hangs thick in the air as I watch Magnolia sleep. Elbows on my knees, head hung low, my eyes lift as I watch the peaceful rise and fall of her chest from across the room. She looks so serene and calm. She smiles in her sleep and our demons retreat further into our dreaded past, if only for a while.

After our confessions, after the last few hours together, I should be feeling as peaceful as she looks. But I don't. I can't let myself. Not when I have a gnawing suspicion that now is not the time to let my guard down, even if doing so welcomes the one thing I've always wanted.

Her.

Death will only come at the hand of my weakness. Something I've feared since the moment I laid eyes on her.

Fuck, I dream of death, because I'd finally be free. Not a prisoner held to a life sentence every waking moment since the day my children's lives were stolen. A pawn, constantly held hostage by the fact that I failed them, and in doing so, I also failed her.

Mathew and Emma, our twins, would've been 17 years old last Thursday. The night we both finally broke in the back seat of that car. Last Thursday was the night we both couldn't take the pain anymore. Put on the same assignment for the first time in seven years, it resurfaced like it did when their deaths were fresh. The only way to silence both our monsters inside was to take it out on each other. The only way we've ever known how. Taking what we want from each other was easy. Loving one another, in spite of both our sins proves much more difficult.

We were both on assignment the night our job went horrifically wrong. A setup for what our target really had in mind. A sick trick to cut us where it mattered most, taking away our strength, our power, our dominance as the most feared team the FBI has to offer and our countries strongest secret weapon.

We'd been tailing the guy for two years and were finally setup to bring him to justice. We'd never seen his face, only blurred out images on street cams, but had a sure tip that led us into a suicide mission that took out many of the bureau's men and women in the process. The sick reality is, he orchestrated an attack that not only took away our children, but in turn, our only sanity. When we found out they were taken, we negotiated a ransom. But the Russian Bratva fucker who stole them in the middle of the night while they were sleeping never intended to keep them alive. A reality we faced after it was already too late.

I begged the FBI to let me take him down. To not negotiate with a man who I was damn sure had no intention of letting them go without one hell of a fight. I was immediately voted down. Overthrown by my superior.

I never should have listened. I should have followed my instinct as every bit of my soul told me to go behind the bureaus back and get my kids back. Free them from the hands of a mad man, no matter what the cost, and get them back into the arms of their mother, even if I died in the process.

By the time I made my move, I realized I had waited mere minutes too long. The Bratva bastard got away, and I'll never forgive myself for that. His perfectly constructed plan was an empty house as screams echoed through speakers taking me further inside until I found the backroom where a video played on loop. The main attraction, a sight that stole the heart out of my chest and brought me to my knees as I watched my children slowly die on screen.

I'll never forget the look of panic, of fear, as it crept across my wife's face when she arrived, stumbling into that back room, and we realized our mistake too late. When we understood we'd been fucking played.

Good thing is, I'm all the wiser now.

"Declan," I hear Magnolia whisper in her sleep. "Please, don't...not again. Don't leave me again."

She rolls on her side, unsettled in her dreams and my heart physically aches watching her and remembering all that we've been through. The sheet falls low in her restlessness, baring her perfect tits and my mouth waters instinctively as I focus on her blush-colored nipples. Perky. Begging for me to lick, suck, nibble on their tips and bring us both more pleasure. But the nightmare inside me screams too loud right now to set me free to do so.

How could I leave her? She's all I have left. All I've ever wanted. My life started and ended with her that hellish night. Even though I'm sentenced to walk through purgatory now, waiting for the day I can finally set us both free, I could never walk away from her. Hell, I could never leave her side for one-second ever again if it meant her fate might mirror our children's.

Two truths and a lie.

Fuck.

More like three sins and a death wish. Three sins I'm destined to fuckup, one way or another. No matter how hard I try.

As I sit in the dark and stare at the one thing that makes me most vulnerable in life, my beautiful Godsend wife, I wrestle with the idea that maybe we can love each other again. Maybe we can try. Possibly start over. Even with our fucked-up past and our undetermined future. If she'll have me.

Once upon a time.

Hell, more like once upon a nightmare.

Fuck once upon a time. The problem with that bullshit is it brings you full circle as you find yourself drowning in the thing you're trying hardest to escape - the past.

My cell vibrates on silent as it sits on the table next to me, pulling me from my thoughts. I pick it up quickly and accept the call.

"Does she suspect anything," Kira questions as I lean back in my chair and study her peaceful frame from across the room.

"I wouldn't be any good at my job if she did," I hiss in response, then wait to be reprimanded for my insubordination, but it never comes. "Last I checked, this call wasn't supposed to take place until 1430. What gives, Kira?"

"We've received rumors the job we've requested you accomplish is compromised."

"By who?" I grit out, my annoyance growing as her heavy sigh follows. It fills the line and makes me furious as I wait for Kira to tell me whose neck I need to break next.

Working as a double agent has its perks and its disadvantages, and is the one secret I've kept hidden from my wife since the night our lives ended. Coming full circle, disclosing both my two lies and one truth, it looks like all my secrets have been revealed. *Or have they?* If my assignment to gain intel on the Chinese government in order to stop their economic espionage fails because of a rat, so does my job to bring back information on the Russian military to Kira. In exchange for my information, Kira has agreed to give me some very important, highly classified details on the whereabouts of my children's killer.

"I'd like to tell you that information isn't your concern, however," she pauses, her voice hanging in the air, grating on my last nerve as I watch and observe Magnolia starting to stir. "Your wife may like to play more tricks than you remember, 0013," Kira asserts, making all the blood in my veins turn ice cold. I stare at my wife in the darkness and wonder if all we just confessed was done so in vain. "You might want to start frisking her first for wires. You know, before you decide to fuck her."

"Last time I checked, it wasn't a crime to sleep with your own wife."

"But aiding and abetting the enemy *is*, Ace," Kira fumes a second later.

"You know what they say," I hiss, releasing a heavy sigh. "Keep your friends close and your enemies closer."

"If these rumors turn out to be true," she snaps, "you stand to lose the last thing that you care about in the entire world. The only thing that's kept you sane these last seven years, Ace; the one thing that's stopped you from losing it all. Information only I can give you."

"And how will you ever find out about Magnolia?" I snap back with disdain, because there's no way in hell she can be right. "The only one she's working this job with, is me, Kira. The only one she's close to, is me. I keep a closer eye on her than she keeps on herself."

"Are you sure about that?"

Magnolia rolls to her side and then slowly sits up in bed. Her eyes remain closed for a moment as she stretches her arms above her head. I watch her in the darkness and wait, her eyes gracefully open a second later and appear only slightly startled as she adjusts to her surroundings; to the weight of what transpired a few hours ago on the bed she's sitting on. She looks up at me and my heart slams to the pit of my stomach, anger turning the ice in my veins into a homicidal fire as I take in what Kira says next.

"Find out who the rat is, 0013, before it finds you." My grip tightens on the phone as my wife attempts a smile at me from across the room.

"What is it?" she innocently asks. Instinctively, I let my mind go numb in order to block both of the women out so I can focus on how much I might be fucked.

"Report back to headquarters before midnight," my superior demands. "Or we'll take the only thing you love most and erase your plan for vengeance before it ever got started." When I don't answer, blinded by the revelation of what I just heard, and desperately not wanting to believe it, Kira goes on. "Want to know the best part, Ace?" My grip on my phone turns brutal as my teeth grind together in a murderous madness and I stare into my wife's wide eyes. "You won't even see us coming."

The line goes dead, and I sit stunned, fighting with the fact that could ruin it all. Kira just may be right. No one's wanted to ruin me more over the last several years than the woman sitting across from me now. The one demanding answers with her eyes like the woman who just called and aggressively handed me an ultimatum I'll refuse to accept.

They both forget who they're dealing with. Good thing for all of us, I have no problem reminding them. My mission has always been to seek full restitution for a wrong I was forced to commit. This isn't over until I receive a full pardon.

Until everyone pays for their sins.

WEDNESDAY

11:25 P.M.

"Fuck man, I swear on all things holy I have no clue what you're talking about!" Timmy screams as I pull the knife from my waist and take a step closer in the darkness. I glance to my right and take in my wife's pleading eyes as she struggles to break free from her restraints.

"Declan, please..."

Slap!

Her head rolls back to the left as my fist collides with her cheek. The chair she's sitting on rocks backward and Timmy's screams only escalate to a piercing high as I take a step forward and grab Magnolia's chin in my hand. Her eyes lock with my own, pissed, scared, and confused. Unfortunately for both of them, I can see we have a long way to go in this interrogation before any of us gets anywhere near the truth.

"Shit, man, you just hit your wife," Timmy screeches. "What

kind of a fucked-up monster does that?" He attempts to scoot back in the chair I tied him to an hour ago and only manages to almost tumble to the side in the process. I rub my thumb down the side of my wife's now red face before staring in her eyes and trying to tell her without words exactly how I feel.

Pain is temporary. What we need to uncover here promises to bring more suffering before their time is inevitably up. I dragged Magnolia's ass out of bed and wrestled her into her restraints after my call with Kira. Tying her partially naked form up with the intent to finally understand what they're both hiding, I groan as I look down and see her tits pressed tight against the rope, straining out of her lacy nightgown.

None of us will be going anywhere until I am sure each and every truth that's hiding is out in the open.

"There's no pleasure without a little pain, Timmy," I hiss, looking down my wife's frame and knowing she's not wearing any panties under the lacy fabric that's riding up her thighs. "No enjoyment without a few agonizing moments of suffering. All before it finally becomes brutally clear."

My hand falls from her cheek and I caress down her neck, enjoying the fresh fire brewing in her eyes as I tighten my grip around her throat. Her breathing comes in sharp spurts as I fan the flames, my fingers pulling down slowly on the top of her lace nightgown.

Interesting.

"I told you, I didn't call anyone," Timmy yells. "I didn't tell anyone...anything! I swear. I don't even have my phone. You've had me locked up in that room for almost two days now, who could I have called..."

"You were alone for almost an hour when you retrieved the satellite feeds," I insist with fresh vengeance for the truth as my wife's eyes stay cold and detached. My head turns as my gaze locks with his terrified one. "You took your sweet time, Timmy," I insist, as I rise back up from Magnolia's side and take a step in his direction. "Slowly downloading what we needed to disc. You signaled three times for help, and then, miraculously, acquired what you needed only moments before we could get to you."

"I...I... didn't. I..."

"For fuck sakes, Tim," I groan in annoyance as I take another step in his pathetic direction. "I'm getting really damn tired of that stutter."

In one quick flick of my wrist, I pull him towards me and angle my knife at his throat. The kid bounces around in his seat, like a damn animated grasshopper, and I almost lose all control and have to force myself not to cut him before I get answers.

His eyes meet Magnolia's behind me, and just the thought of them in cahoots sends a painful burn rushing straight to my damned heart. I look behind me quickly to see the way her eyes look in their exchange, but she gives nothing away. Only stares back at me blankly. Ready to meet any fate necessary.

With my eyes trained on Magnolia's, I push the blade into little Timmy's neck and watch to see if she cares. To see if she's playing me. Hell, maybe even playing him. But she sits frozen. Unaffected. So, I push my blade into his skin a little bit more, listen as he screams out and a small amount of blood trickles onto my wrist.

"Ok, ok!" he finally yells, making both Magnolia and my eyes flash to his. "What if, I could find out who for you?"

My mind struggles to keep up with his quick change of heart as my brow furrows and I wait for him to continue.

"What if, I could find out what happened?"

"I don't care about what happened, Timmy," I seethe, as I lean in closer and pull the blade slowly across the base of his neck, just enough to barely break through his skin. He tries to disguise his cries as his bottom lip quivers, but they eventually blubber over, spurting out of his mouth like a pitiful fountain. "I care who did it! I want to know where they live. When they sleep. When they're taking a shit!"

His eyes close, and thicker, aggravating, whimpers escape his lips. His chair starts rocking again, this time quicker than before. Rising quickly, I stomp my boot in between his legs, barely missing his dick, in order to stop the bouncing. His shrill yell assaults my ears as he looks down, scared for a manhood he doesn't fucking possess, and it only pisses me off more.

We're far from getting answers here and I only have so much patience. Especially when there's a high price on the line and time is running out before I lose everything I've been working towards for the last seven years.

"I don't remember a name," Timmy shakes his head, but then closes his eyes and attempts to concentrate.

Try harder, Tim. Your life depends on it.

"But," he shrieks, as his eyes open and he once again starts to stutter. "I...I remember... I remember them talking about Russia."

Instinctively I look back at Magnolia as her eyes widen, a small break in the otherwise always stone exterior. A trick of her trade that's never failed her on the job, until now. But hearing you might be close to the vengeance you seek after all these years will do that to you. I hold Magnolia's eyes for a moment and watch as her breathing increases. A sweat breaks out across her flawless skin and she grows pale. Tears prick the backs of her eyes and I grind my teeth in bitterness because I can tell both of us are thinking the same damn thing.

"Is... is that wrong," he expels on a shaky breath as I slowly turn my heated gaze back towards him. Timmy glances in her direction and then frantically looks back at me. "No...no I know I am right. I heard what they said," he stutters again. "I swear it."

"No," I hiss, as my molars grind. "That's got to be right, Tim. After all, you heard what they said. No bullshitting. No fucking around. Right?"

He shakes his head in agreement, like the chump he is, and I shake mine back, telling him no, just to fuck with him. There's something in his eyes I don't trust. There is something here that is not adding up. And I'm determined to figure out what he's hiding.

"When was this?"

"Last week," he quickly says. "Two nights before I met you. Two nights before..."

"What time?"

"Fuck, I don't know what time." I lean in and press the tip of my blade against his cock, applying just enough pressure to scare the shit out of him, but not enough to cause him too much damage. *Yet.* "9...9 o'clock. Fuck, 9:30. I don't know, it was dark outside. I remember that."

"You said them? How many were there?"

"Two, maybe three. It was hard to tell, it was pitch black in that alley. I wouldn't have even been there if I didn't have to piss. But the line was too long to get into the club, and..."

I drown him out as he stammers on. My mind racing, knowing that I could've caught the fuckers that stole away both mine and Magnolia's life seven years ago last week if I hadn't been holding my wife's face down in the back of that damn car, drowning in heartache when I should have been seeking vengeance.

But, shit, if they cornered our friend Timmy in that alley, they must have seen us there too. So why didn't they take us out when they had the chance? Why fuck with us even more? With our life one time was enough. But twice? There's more to this than any of us know and I'm getting a fucked-up sense of Deja vu the longer I stand here talking to our little friend.

"Did they take you anywhere, Tim?" I hiss. "Did you leave with them?" It would explain why Timmy was MIA that night and we had to locate him a few days later.

"They took me to an empty warehouse on Second Street," he eagerly says. Too eagerly. It gives him away, and gives me an idea.

"Do you think you can remember how to get there?"

"I..I can try." He looks back at Magnolia as if she'll praise him again for a job well done. He's more of a fool than I originally thought. Walking back over to my wife, I cut her restraints and help her out of the chair. Timmy's eyes grow wide as I brush the hair back away from her face and study the redness I inflicted there.

"How's the cheek?" I whisper, ignoring the rat next to us as he pathetically starts to struggle against the ropes that bind him. Leaning in, I take her face in my palms and study the side of her face. The one I never thought I'd hit in my whole damn life, and the one Magnolia told me to smack while I was tying her up if it meant getting the information we needed. "I swore I'd never lay a finger on you Sweetheart that wasn't meant to bring you the most pleasure. This red mark, right here," I whisper, brushing my hand gently against her skin, "doesn't make me happy."

"Who's to say I didn't enjoy it."

Shaking my head, I smile. "Who's the masochist now, Mags?"

I look down into little Timmy's eyes and shake my head, telling him to stop the bullshit. He's not free to go. The only way to end this is with vengeance for a life that was stolen, and with going forward with the original plan.

The one I told my wife about right before I dragged her in here, told her to play along, and then tied her beautiful, breathtaking ass to the chair behind me.

"I could find them, if you want me to," Timmy cries. "Just please, please. I don't want to die."

Funny Tim. That's all I've wanted for seven fucking years. Until tonight.

"I'm not going to kill you," I rasp out, stepping away from my wife and moving closer to where he sits. When he still doesn't look convinced, I shake my head and say, "Hell, Tim. I thought we'd become better friends than that. You're hurting my feelings."

He stares at me in shock. Entirely not believing me until I slowly walk behind his chair, untie his wrists, and give him the freedom he never thought he'd walk away with. When I'm done, I walk towards my wife. My eyes holding hers the entire time and knowing that what we started tonight, our new beginning, runs deeper with the knowledge that the one fucker we've been hunting down since *that* day seven years ago is now closer than we ever thought possible.

As my fingers brush against my wife's skin and I slip her hand into mine, a sort of hopeful faith filled me inside. We've atoned for our sins. It's time they paid for theirs.

"Wha...what do we do now?" Timmy stammers at our side as I take my wife's hand and place a tender kiss against her wrist. She smiles at me as I release her hand, and reach behind my back.

"For starters," I smile, as I pull my Sig from its holster and take aim. "You take us to this warehouse, Tim. You have no idea who you're fucking with, so let me enlighten you. You stepped into a war you have no chance of winning. People are going to die tonight. Better start praying you're not one of them."

***

11:45 p.m.

"I have the rat," I hiss into my phone as I push Timmy towards the backdoor of the warehouse. "Although, I can't promise I'll keep him alive after I finish off his friends. Looks like I didn't need you after all, Kira."

"I have men on the ground, covering you, Ace. Unless you want me to tell them to back off?"

"Put them on Magnolia. Anything happens to her; I'm coming after you next."

"Is that a threat."

"It's a fucking promise." I end the call and shove the phone back in my pocket. Giving our little friend Timmy a slight push with the barrel of my gun, I grin as he anxiously makes his way towards the back door.

"Wha...what about me?" He stammers. "Who covers me?"

"You, Tim?" I laugh. "No one's covering you. Fuck, didn't you know? You're the pawn, Timmy." I hiss into his ear as he slowly opens the back door. "Disposable. Expendable. A puppet, whose strings have been pulled for the very last time."

He stumbles over the doorstep as I hold him like a human shield with my gun held to his spine. The warehouse is pitch black, the only light shining in from small windows located all around the buildings 30-foot ceilings. It's quiet. Too quiet. An eerie nightmare come to life as I take advantage of the silence when I hear a slight noise to my left and swing Timmy around to face it.

The low whistle of the silencer registers seconds before Timmy's body goes rigid in my arms. His death happens so fast he doesn't even have time to scream. A first maybe for our little rat friend, and I feel only a tiny bit guilty for his death as I release him and watch him drop to the floor.

The whistle of the silencer lightly pierces through the darkness again, as I barely have time to jump behind a nearby crate for cover. Timmy said there was two of them, maybe three, and my heart rate spikes as I look up, before glancing to both sides and making sure I'm not under an attack.

A light flicks on overhead and I still. I stop fucking breathing. Waiting. Mentally preparing for the worst and praying for the best.

A low laugh fills the room a second later. A woman's laugh and my heart stops. Clapping rings through the large space, bouncing off the concrete walls and echoing through to the pit of my stomach. *What the hell?* I cock my gun, hold it high and take aim as I push off the crate and turn to face my fate.

The sound of the silencer weaves through the air and I duck, barely missing the bullet. Looking up, I take aim and land my shot right in the center of his skull. One down. One, possibly two more to go. I weave through more crates and catch a glimpse of my next opponent. Picking up my pace, I round the corner and don't hesitate, landing a shot right at the base of his neck.

Timidly, I glance around me and walk slowly through the rest of the maze. The woman's low laugh echoes once again off the walls around me and making me realize where we went wrong. We were never looking for the man from the weak surveillance videos. But a girl. A woman. And as I recognize the sound of her voice my blood turns ice cold because this *little one* played games with the wrong fucking people.

Sandra Winslow.

Or should I say Goldilocks.

Timmy was fucking with us from the start. Suddenly, I feel a whole lot less guilty over his death as I stare Goldilocks in the eyes and take a slow, calculated step forward.

"Very good," her accent is thick as she smiles, her hands raise and her claps of sheer enjoyment ring through the space around us.

"You're Russian," I state the obvious, my breathing labored as I take another step forward. "Sandra..."

"Victoria," she states with authority as her smile turns to stone. Her eyes glaze over, and she studies me as I take another step forward. "Sokolov. Maybe it's you that can't handle me, 0013."

My eyebrows raise as I question just how she knows about my double identity.

"Oh, don't be so shocked, Ace," she laughs. "It was easy. We'd known Kira was looking into hiring the FBI's most deadly weapon to spy on our military intelligence. How best to stop him, but to take away what he loves most? A loss that would drop him to his knees and make him weak. Defenseless and useless. Blinded by vengeance and incapable of seeing a rat, even when it was right under his nose."

Motion catches my eyes to the right and I raise my gun, taking aim quickly, only to drop it back to my side a moment later as the world stops spinning.

Mathew. Emma.

I take off towards them. It's been seven years, but I've seen pictures of them over time. I knew they were still alive. A fact I never told Magnolia for fear I'd fail her again.

Victoria holds up her hand and I stop, but only because the sick fuck who's brought them back out into the light after all this time has a gun pointed straight at my daughter's head. The prick behind him no doubt has another pointed at my son's back from the panic reflected in his eyes.

"Deception is easiest played on the most powerful," Victoria insists as my eyes stay locked on my children's. "You believe in your strength so much; you never take the time to truly see what makes you weak."

My daughter's tears fall over as her lip quivers in horror. I look to my son and see him visibly trembling, his fear causing him to cry out, saying the name I never thought I'd hear again for the rest of my damned life. *"Dad."* I plead with them to hold on. This will all be over soon. I won't fail them this time.

Glancing back at Victoria, a faint glimmer behind her catches my eye as I release a deep breath, filled with years of built up vengeance, glare at her and say, "The strongest man is the one who embraces his weakness."

Her gasp is loud as the knife raises to her throat and I watch as Magnolia's hand quickly pulls it across her skin. I don't watch a second longer, I know all too well what's spilled at the hands of my wife. Sweet revenge we've waited seven damn years for.

Glancing back to my right, I take aim and shoot the bastard that has his gun pressed to my daughter's temple. He stumbles back, taking her with him and they both fall to the floor. I rush forward and hear a shot ring out a moment later.

My heart stills. My feet stop. The nightmare that I've been running from for seven years rushes back as real as the first day I felt it and I realize my mistake. I failed to protect my son.

THURSDAY

12:30 A.M.

THE PAST only serves one purpose.

To destroy you if you let it.

The truth about a lie is, it's never, really, *truly* a lie, right?

Most everyone's deceit holds a small amount of honesty. A little bit of yourself that could be true, if you let it.

My name is Declan Ace McClintock.

My profession?

Husband. Father.

My first priority is to them forever. Being a hired hitman when needed for the FBI, and a double agent for the United Nations always comes second.

My weakness?

My wife. My children. Always.

Now, I know what you're thinking. My profession's been

exposed. My weakness never stands a chance of being conquered.

But as I look down into my arms, tighten my hold on my daughter and pull my son into my arms a moment later, I couldn't give a fuck if I'm forever handicapped by my weakness. If I lose my job and have to find a new line of work.

I got my life back. I've received absolution for my sins. Delivered a penance and made them pay the ultimate retribution for their own. I received full atonement, finally after seven long years and as I look up in my wife's tear-filled eyes and watch as our children push out of my arms and run into the embrace of their mother.

Mission fucking accomplished.

My earpiece buzzes a moment later and I hear Kira's voice come over the line. "Ace, we've seized control of Victoria's backup plan. Five Bratva members, armed and ready to barge through the back door. As far as I'm concerned, this job never happened. Take a fucking vacation and be ready to report to headquarters in 10 days. Your debt isn't paid off yet."

That's another thing I couldn't give a fuck about. I'll forever be in debt for the job they helped me finish. It's a debt I have no problem paying as my wife rises to her feet, holds my children's hands and walks towards me looking happier than I've seen her in years.

"10.4." I respond, just as she reaches my side and I pull her into my arms, both of us feeling lighter than we have in years.

"Dad," my son's voice calls to me and I swear my heart explodes. "Can we go home now?"

I look down into his eyes, then glance at my daughter who's face still holds panic, fear, shame, and I fear she's forever changed by what she walked through over the years we've been forced to spend apart.

"Yeah, Buddy," I smile softly. "Let's go home."

I catch my wife's eyes as we walk out of the building. She

glances down at our daughter, her hand shaking in her mother's grasp as she looks behind her with terror. She gives me the same worried look I felt grace my face moments ago. Both of us knowing it will take time, but we'll fix this. We'll dedicate our life to helping her get past this. Both of them. Any way we can.

Reaching the car, our children climb into the back seat, almost as if they've been trained to never disobey. I shake my head knowing we have a long road to walk before we can ever put this behind us. If we ever can. But as my gaze rises and I lock eyes with my wife, I smile as she takes a few steps towards me, I pull her close, and savor her kiss. Slowly. Deliberately. Appreciating every slip of her tongue against mine, I drown in our victory before reluctantly pulling away and looking her lovingly in the eye.

"Were you ever going to tell me about Russia?" she bites her lip before pushing back slightly in my arms.

Here we go.

She studies me. Fire returning to those eyes that I love so much to tame. I don't respond, because truth be told, no, I was never planning on telling her, so I never was faced with my worst fear - failing her once again.

"Just because you got me back in your bed, Ace, doesn't mean there can still be secrets between us. Doesn't mean I have to give you everything you want when you're not giving me what I need in return."

"Hm, tell me how that works again," I taunt, tightening my grip on her waist and pulling her closer. "Because, if I remember correctly. I got everything I wanted earlier, without complying to your demands. Your wet pussy. Your tight ass. Only thing I didn't fuck, was your mouth, Sweetheart," her lips part and her jaw drops. "But," I tease, taking her chin in my hand, a mischievous grin spreading across my smug face as her eyes widen. "I can see now that you're willing."

"What you want, Declan, and what I need will always be two separate things."

"Then you can forget about Russia." There's more to that story than she'll ever know. I may have had to blow my cover to successfully pull off the only job that's ever mattered most to us, but I'll be damned if I put her life in jeopardy again if I can guard her from secrets she shouldn't know.

"Then forget about my mouth," she huffs, pushing off my chest with so much angst it has my dick slightly hardening in my slacks. I let her go, lustfully watching her ass sway as she struts around the vehicle to the passenger door.

"There's more places I can put it, Mags," I reprimand her before we open our car doors. "Keep up the attitude, and I'll take you over my damn knee if I have to and show you."

"I'd like to see you fucking try."

Oh, would she?

My eyebrow raises as we silently inflict a standoff against each other once again. After a moment, we quietly agree to stop fighting only to climb into our opposing seats in the car. I look into the backseat just as she does the same. Our life finally back together again, we glance back at each other a moment later and smile. The silence stretches between the four of us as I start the ignition and the Aston Martin comes to life.

"Two truths and a lie, Magnolia," I tease, as I rev the engine and look to my side before glancing in the rearview mirror and taking in the eyes of our children. I hold onto their fearful stare and make them a promise. I'll fix all that went wrong. Like I promised, I won't fail them. Never again.

"What the hell are you taking about, Dec?" my wife's annoyed sigh breaks through my thoughts a second later.

"For starters, Russia," I suggest, as I turn and look her way. "Second. What you really need, Mags, not just what you think you want. Third. Me. Taking what you always deny, even when I know how much you really want it." She stares at me over the center console, her arms folded over her chest. She glares at me with such animosity it fuels a raging fire that heads straight for my dick and I can't help but fucking smile. "You game, Sweetheart?"

"Oh, Ace," she laughs, as I shift the car into first and pull away from the curb. "I'm always game. The question is, are you?"

The End

ABOUT THE AUTHOR

Born and raised in California, Evelyn Montgomery now resides in Central Kentucky with her husband and three children. Writing all types of romance, her novels include love stories that revolve around contemporary, suspenseful, thriller, phycological, comedy and much more.
One thing readers can always expect when reading one of her books is a twist somewhere between the pages they'd never see coming. With over 10 novels currently published, her goal is to keep producing a fictional world that isn't forced, but genuine, heartfelt, and desirable.
To keep in contact, follow Evelyn on one of the platforms below.

Facebook
Instagram
TikTok
Twitter
Mailing List
Website
FB Group
BookBub
Goodreads
Amazon

ACKNOWLEDGEMENTS

First & always foremost.
To my Lord & Savior.
Thank you for blessing me with my passion to write and create,
even if I'm not always perfect in your eyes.
To my husband and children.
Thank you for your continued patience as I build my dream and
think up new worlds I can't wait to bring to life.
Special thanks to Claire Wade and Rachel Nesling on this project.
From the title to edits, you ladies helped quickly bring this
together and I'm forever grateful.
To my readers who've stayed with me through my absence this
last year.
I love you, and thank you.
I hope you're excited for what's to come.
Because we're just getting started!

Made in the USA
Monee, IL
17 May 2022